Looking For Atlantis

I0633181

Mark Magrs

chipmunkapublishing
the mental health publisher

Mark Magrs

Published by
Chipmunkapublishing
PO Box 6872
Brentwood
Essex CM13 1ZT
United Kingdom

http://www.chipmunkapublishing.com

Edited by Marc Wilson

Chipmunkapublishing gratefully acknowledge the support of Arts Council England.

Author's Note

All of the characters and events in this book are fictitious. Any resemblance to actual persons, living or dead is purely coincidental.

Lyrics from '*Looking For Atlantis*' and '*Goodbye Lucille #1*' reproduced by kind permission of Paddy McAloon and Prefab Sprout.

With thanks to Nicki at Kitchenware Records.

The author would like to acknowledge the financial support of the 'New Writing North' Northern Writers' Awards and of the Cultural Sector Development Initiative.

Mark Magrs

Looking For Atlantis

For Brian

Mark Magrs

Looking For Atlantis

Saturday Night

"Get that bloody door closed!"

It's proper cold outside. I can't see any clouds, and there's a bite in the air. It's *perfect*!!!

"Did you hear what I said?" Mam is in the living room, and she's noticed the draft. "Get that door closed before I catch my bloody death!"

"But mam," I say, "it's a totally clear sky – you can see *all* the stars!" I shut the door and head back into the warm.

Mam is sitting in her chair, eyes fixed on the television. It's one of those *'vote for the best singer'* programmes – and she never misses those.

"I don't know what you're playing at," she says to me, without ever looking away from the TV. "Opening the back door on a night like this…" She tuts loudly.

Our living room is small and L-shaped with a deep red carpet and far too much furniture. Mam has tables for her knick-knacks, ornaments, paper-weights and lamps. She collects those brightly coloured figures of old-fashioned ladies, the ones with big dresses and skinny arms. They're made out of porcelain and I always think I'm going to knack them when I do the dusting. Most of the walls are taken up with shelves so she can show them off. God knows why – she never lets anyone in here. It's a good job we can't afford to re-decorate 'cos I don't know where we'd put them all while I scraped off the wallpaper.

"I told you what I was looking for," I tell her, "I did say – it was on the news…" Mam doesn't watch the news 'cos of all the murder and terrorism. She says it makes her miserable. I never miss it.

"Sshhh – he's coming on now…"

If she could, my mam would always vote for the bloke with the croaky voice and the long hair. He's always singing Bryan Adams songs – and my mam *loves* Bryan Adams. I don't know how singing like that is supposed to be good. He sounds like I did when I had tonsillitis. The people who go on those programmes only ever choose from about five different songs and they always seem to be about being in love or being sad 'cos someone they were in love with has died. I once asked mam why these people never sing anything a bit different or why they can't write their own songs, but she just glared at me. She sits, wrapped up in her cardigan and comfy track-suit bottoms, dunking a biscuit in her cup of tea with her eyes stuck to the telly. I sit on the settee and wait for the hairy bloke to finish croaking.

This is our regular Saturday night. Every Friday afternoon my nanna goes home to see her friends and play bingo and I do my best to keep mam company 'til I go back to school on Monday. We sit in front of the telly eating biscuits and drinking tea. Mam sometimes sees the way I look at her when she opens another packet of chocolate digestives and she'll say something like:

"Oh leave me alone, it's my only pleasure in life!" before taking a big bite. It's all right for her, she won't put weight on no matter how much she eats – but my school trousers aren't half getting tight around my middle.

My brother's away at University and he stopped coming home to visit after the first term – mam says he's so busy with exams that he doesn't have time to come and see us – but he's probably just spent all his money on beer or woolly hats like all students do. Nanna says that *I* am the '*man of the house*' when she's not here. She always laughs after she says that – and I really don't know why. She might be laughing because she doesn't think I'm a man (and I'm only fourteen so that's fair enough), or she's laughing at the idea of her being a man. Either way, it's more weird than funny, if you ask me.

Looking For Atlantis

My mam actually applauds at the end of the croaky bloke's song. I've tried to tell her that it's pretty pointless clapping a TV show, but she doesn't listen. She almost seems to enjoy doing it – and the more I complain the more she does it. I wait for the next lot of adverts before I talk to her.

"I told you I was going out in the garden tonight," I say.

"Yes and I told you not to be so bloody daft."

"But it'll never happen again!" Mam doesn't reply to this comment, she just exhales loudly. "It's a once in a lifetime thing, they reckon it happens once every two thousand years and I thought that was dead interesting! Just think – Jesus was alive the last time that comet came past. He might've watched it, too!"

Mam turns to look at me with a big frowny expression on her face.

"Yes," she says, "but he lived somewhere a lot bloody warmer than us!" She turns back to the telly. Mam always says that she doesn't swear, but she does. I've heard her say all sorts of things – especially when she talks to nanna about my dad.

I take a key with me. I'm going to go and watch for the comet, even if she's not interested. This is the sort of thing I can tell people about one day – maybe when I'm an old man like my nanna. I suppose that's why people keep diaries; in case they forget stuff like this.

Mam hears me opening the door again - the clicking of the lock.

"You must be mad!" she laughs. I can hear her moving from her chair – she's not supposed to do that! I turn back, and she's making a grab for her sticks. If she falls flat on her face I'll get into trouble. Especially if I laugh.

"Mam, what are you doing?"

"I want to see what all this fuss is about," she grumbles as I take her arm.

I feel guilty and move to help her back towards her chair.

"I'll only be outside for a minute," I say, "you watch your programme, they'll be doing the voting soon."

"I've seen me boyfriend now," she says, "help me out in the chair".

"Are you sure, mam?"

"Just do it – before I change my bloody mind!"

I manage to avoid scraping any more paint off the door frame as I wheel mam to the back door in her chair. She reminds me to be careful as I lift the front over the door-step and then use the handles to bump the wheel chair down onto the garden path.

"The grass needs cutting," she says and she's right. In fact, the whole garden is a mess. It'll have to wait til Spring now. Maybe Nanna will help.

Our breath is all fluffy in the air around us. It suddenly feels very quiet – as if the traffic that should be on the main road has all gone and the other houses seem to be a million miles away.

"Is that it?" Mam blurts out suddenly. Right up above us – in amongst the blues and the blacks and the purples of the sky - there is a tiny flicker. It looks like somebody has lit a candle on the other side of the universe. It's so far away – further than Australia. It's not very spectacular.

"Aye." I try to sound enthusiastic. "Just think – two thousand years it takes to come round." Mam doesn't answer. She just stares.

I don't like it when she's quiet. I always feel as if I'm doing something wrong.

We both stare at that tiny flicker in outer space without saying anything. I wonder how many other people are looking at it all over the world. Probably not many from our town, but there must be people out there with telescopes and binoculars – all getting a glimpse of something that they'll never see again.

I can just see some clouds appearing at the edges of the night sky – they look like they're starting to chase the stars away.

"Come on mam," I say, "let's get you back inside." I grab the handles of the wheel-chair and start lifting the front wheels over the door-step. My mam has gone very quiet. "It *is* too cold to stay out this long." I try to make a joke of it, but she doesn't answer.

The living room seems smaller than ever as we come back in. Mam is still quiet as I sit her back in front of the telly. I don't know how long we were outside but the adverts are finished and there are some singing twins on the telly.

I say to mam:

"Do you want another cup of tea?" We've still got quite a few biscuits to get through.

Letter to the Mayor Number 1

46 Sampson Place
Newton Aycliffe
County Durham

Dear Mrs. Rutter,

I realise that you must be a very busy person, what with the council meetings, public lunches and school assemblies that you have to go to, but I have a really good idea that could make a big difference to lots of people. I would've rang you up but my mam hasn't got the phone on at the moment, so I thought I'd write instead.

It was on the news last night about a famine in Africa. People are saying that if something isn't done then millions of Africans are going to starve this Winter. It made me think because in our town, I often see a man begging outside of the old closed-down Woolworths and from the looks of him he might starve this Winter, too.

I'm sure that you and the other members of our town council have lots of ideas about what to do in situations like this, but I've thought of something that might help.

I was in town quite late the other night – I'd been in the Library doing my homework – and most of the shops were closing. Anyway, I was heading for the bus stop when I noticed some of the women who work in PJ's Bakery putting big bags into a giant sized wheelie bin. When I asked them what they were doing they told me that they have to throw out all of the stuff that doesn't get sold! And it's true. I asked their boss. I watched them do it. Just after five o'clock every day they throw bags and bags of food away – loaves of bread, pasties, cream cakes, sausage rolls, meat pies, chicken pies, the lot! They make fresh stuff every day so they always have too much! I asked them why they didn't offer some of it to the man who begs outside of the old closed-down Woolworths and they told me that they aren't allowed to.

I don't know if you are aware of this, but every bakery in town does the same thing – I know because I've been and watched. I have tried to tell them that they should give the food to hungry people (in our country and abroad) but they always say that they can't. They never seem to have a very good reason why they don't do it, they just don't. They even put padlocks on the bins to stop people from taking the stuff they don't want! It's outrageous, if you ask me. Anyway, I can't make them give the food away – but maybe you could!

Just imagine if every bakery in our town gave their spare food away – you could feed every hungry person in the county and maybe have some left over to send to Africa as well!

What do you think?

If you want me to, I could give you a list of all the bakeries in town, then you could write to them and make them give their spare food to people who really need it. At the moment, it's all just going into wheelie-bins.

Yours sincerely
Christopher Mason

Monday at School

Today went pretty well. I mean, it went pretty well for a school day.

The morning was boring because we had Geography and Maths. I'm crap at Maths and Mr. Lightly never lets me forget that my brother got an 'A' for his A Level. I don't know what he expects me to do about it, I'm still two years away from doing my GCSE's, so it's not like I can win that race, can I? And Geography is mainly just copying out of books. Mr. McPherson acts as if he doesn't want to speak to us so he just writes a load of page numbers on the board and tells us to get on with it.

I was up in plenty of time before school, so I made sure mam had all of her tablets and was comfortable in the sitting room. I made her a flask of tea so that she wouldn't have to keep going backwards and forwards to the kitchen, and I even checked that the batteries were still working in the TV remote control. I don't want to give her any more excuses to moan at me. Mam reckons she never watches any day-time telly but she always seems to know what's been going on in the Australian soaps and those programmes about families who keep fighting with each other. I hoped she'd be OK until nanna got back at noon-ish.

Anyway, the day got better after dinner because we had double English and Miss. Hobbs made us work in groups. We had to write a script based on one of the chapters in '*Jane Eyre*'. I usually hate stuff like that. Miss Hobbs only seems to have three ideas; write a diary for one of the characters, write a letter from one of the characters to their mother or write a script based on one of the important bits. I've often thought about telling Miss. Hobbs about my letters, but she'd probably be more concerned about my spelling and grammar

– instead of thinking about what I was saying. My brother used to get Miss. Hobbs for English, too – and she always asks about him. He's doing an English Degree and he used to be her star pupil. Some days, I think he still is.

Today was good, though, because some of us were allowed to work in the corridor so we'd have more room.

Miss. Hobbs actually put us in '*mixed*' groups because she reckons lads never want to work with lasses and if she lets us choose our own groups we'll just end up chatting all the time.

All we did was chat anyway.

I don't really remember much of what we did but it ended up being a brilliant lesson because I was working with David, Janice and the new girl in our class – Nikki. David and Janice are always funny because they really like each other but they spend all of their time trying to prove that they don't. David calls Janice "*her ladyship*", and Janice calls him a "*peasant*." They sometimes use words that I have to look up in a dictionary. Nikki and I just had a good laugh at them. And I got to hear a bit about her, too.

Nikki's family moved down from Scotland in the Summer Holidays but she doesn't have a Scottish accent. She has an older brother – but he's at University so she doesn't see much of him.

"Her family must be rich," David whispered to me, "rich people in Scotland always have English accents."

Nikki said her mam hates living in our town and wants to move back to Scotland as soon as possible. If it wasn't for the fact that we have important exams this year, Nikki reckons her mam would've moved them all back already. They live on the new estate near the school. My mam calls them the '*posh houses*' because you have to get a mortgage to live there instead of paying the council, so maybe David's right about Nikki's family being rich. I kept trying to work out who she reminded me of. She must look like someone off the telly – there's something very familiar about her face. She has long, straight, browny-red hair, pale blue eyes and her skin is very smooth. She doesn't look as if she's ever had any spots. Not like the rest of us.

We spent most of our time talking about the Geography field trip. This weekend we're spending two nights at a Youth Hostel in the Lake District. The idea is that we climb some mountains and cook our own meals – but most people are looking forward to it anyway.

"Ollie and Parky reckon they've got a bottle of vodka," Janice told us, "they think they're going to have some sort of party!"

"I'll just be happy just to see some different scenery..." I said, not talking about the trouble I had getting my mam to let me go.

"McPherson is driving the mini-bus so that should be funny." David chuckled at the thought of it. "He's a total stress head!" Mr McPherson has been known to tear pages out of exercise books if one word is spelt wrong – and his curly hair seems to get tighter and tighter the angrier he gets. "We'll probably see all kinds of road rage."

Miss. Hobbs is coming on the trip because she wants us to visit Dove Cottage on the way home this Sunday. Miss. Hobbs is almost the exact opposite of McPherson in that she never ever seems to get angry. In fact, it's often quite difficult to understand what she's saying because she whispers all the time.

"What the hell's Dove Cottage?" David asked.

"William Wordsworth used to live there," Janice said, "so it's bound to be boring." Janice always pretends that she finds school stuff boring, but that's just because she's so good at it.

After all that, we had to tell the rest of the class what we'd 'found out' about the characters in '*Jane Eyre*'. David and Janice are good at making that stuff up at the last minute, so it was OK, but Miss. Hobbs didn't like it because I said the ending wasn't very realistic. I said that the writer wimped out.

The characters all pretty much got what they wanted (apart from that poor crazy woman in who lived in an attic) and life isn't like that. Miss. Hobbs sighed at me and looked disappointed. She said that I should have another read of '*Jane Eyre*' to see if I've missed something important – but it's such hard work getting through the old-fashioned words. It seems like it's about someone a million miles and a million years away from where we are now.

I remember when my brother did an essay about '*Jane Eyre*' and got full marks for it off Miss. Hobbs. He came home and told me and mam that it was the first time an English Teacher had given anybody full marks for an essay at our school. My mam was going to get his essay framed!

I hate some of the books we have to read in English. The teachers try to find stories about kids so that we'll be interested – but most of the time they haven't got much to do with us. And some of them just aren't realistic at all. '*Jayne Eyre*' is about a young woman – but how many people in our school live a life like hers? She never got picked on for having spots and she certainly never got hassled by teachers for wearing too much make-up.

Last year, when we had Mrs. Verity, she made us read a book about a teenager who found talking animals in the trees behind his house – but nobody believed him. In fact, his mam took him to see a Doctor because she thought her son was '*disturbed*' or something. Up to that point, I thought it was pretty realistic because that's the sort of thing my mam would do. But of course, by the end of the book, all of the adults came to realise that the kid was telling the truth and he had this big adventure in a land of talking animals. I mean, for God's sake. All of the adults had to accept that there *was* magic in the world and that kids are brilliant. The thing that got me, though, was the teacher in the story. The kid in the book had this really friendly, understanding and well-meaning teacher who believed in him. What a load of crap! None of my teachers are like that – they always say they're too busy to talk before running off to the staff-room to drink gallons of coffee. That's why their breaths stink.

I've got nothing against books – I just wish they wouldn't write books for kids that show the world as a wonderful place all the time.

The very best part of the day came just after the bell went for home-time. It turns out that Nikki walks the same way home as me! Most people head out of the main school gates – but some of us go out over the playing fields and through the little wooden fence. That fence runs right round the outside of the school grounds – but most of it has been kicked in so that you can take a short-cut down the hill and onto the path and bridge across the burn. In the Summer Holidays the school always pays to have the fence mended but by half past eight on the first day back it's all in bits again. The hill's a bit muddy, but if you stay on the grass you can cut about fifteen minutes off the walk home!

Anyway – I saw Nikki walking the same way as me. She was wearing a white coat with a brown collar – and I saw her bright red school bag over her shoulder. I was going to shout and ask her to wait so that I could walk with her – but I didn't. I think I like her, but I never know if people like me or not. It's weird – I mean, lots of people my age have girl-friends and boy-friends but I've never been able to work out how that happens. I could ask her out – but where would I take her? There's not a lot round here except a broken down play park and a couple of bus shelters that smell of wee.

Anyway, I didn't shout after because I didn't want her to think that I was following her or stalking her or something.

Letter To Auntie Pat

46 Sampson Place
Newton Aycliffe
County Durham

Dear Auntie Pat,

How are you? It seems to be ages since we spoke on the phone – I think it was two Christmases ago – hopefully we'll have our phone back on by next year.

School is going really well – I got a good report - apart from in P.E. as usual but who cares about that? Ha ha!

Anyway, I thought I'd drop you a line because my mam wanted to write a letter but she hasn't been too good lately. She hopes that you and the family are doing well. She says she's really jealous of all the sunshine you must be getting out there – she watches those Australian soaps on day-time telly and she says you must spend a fortune on sun-tan lotion! We both really wish that we could come and visit you and maybe we will when mam starts to feel a bit better.

Rob hasn't been home lately, and we can't ring him because we haven't got the phone on at the moment. He does send mam letters sometimes and he seems to be working very hard – reading lots of books and writing lots of essays.

Mam and I have to go to the hospital tomorrow (Wednesday) and if it's good news I'll let you know and we can start thinking about the best time for us to come and visit. We should probably come in the Winter so that we can miss all the bad weather at home.

Mam says we probably won't be able to afford to come over – the flights are really expensive – but I'm sure we'll be able to sort something out. It's important that families make time for each other and stick together. It really will be great to see you all!

I'd better go – I have Science homework to do, and I still haven't got my head around peristalsis!
Lots of love

Chris.

Looking For Atlantis

Tuesday at Home

"Haven't you got anything better to do with your time?" Brian snorts. "I mean, it's one thing taping a few albums, most people do that, but making your own covers?" I didn't think it was such a strange thing to do, but Bri seems really freaked out. "It must take you ages!" He's looking at the shelves in my room. "Don't you ever get any homework?" Brian is always getting into trouble for not doing his homework, so I don't know what he's on about with that comment.

"I doesn't take *that* long, once you get started..." He picks up my copy of *'From Langley Park to Memphis'* by Prefab Sprout. I'm really proud of the cover for that one – I managed to get it photo-copied onto coloured paper at the library down town.

"And some of the stuff you like," he says, "this came out before you were born!" I've put my tape collection together by getting stuff out of the library – and rooting through all the old vinyl that my dad left behind. My brother took some of them away to University with him – he picked out the David Bowie and Pink Floyd albums – he doesn't have a record player so he sticks the covers on his wall.

Brian has loads of CDs. He's always copying them for other kids at school, *'burning'* them on his computer or loading them onto mp3 players. He has all the latest stuff – he even manages to get stuff before it comes out in the shops – he says you can find anything on the internet if you know where to look. He's got a lap-top, broadband, one of them photo-taking music playing mobile phones, the lot. Brian is the youngest in his family. He has brothers and sisters in their late twenties and they all give him pocket money every week. He's been spoilt, basically. My mam always says I've been spoilt but I don't know how she dares.

"This must be an antique – can you still get needles for it?" Brian is amazed that I have a record player. It's in a large glass fronted cabinet in the corner of my room. It must be over twenty years old and it has a rack in the bottom for keeping L.P.s in. Mam lets me keep it in my room because she says it's old-fashioned and ugly. But really, she doesn't like it because dad left it behind. Maybe she feels the same way about me.

"I've got a couple of spares, so if I'm careful they should last a while yet." I love getting home from school and putting records on. I've placed the big old chunky speakers of the record player at either side of my bed, so I can lie down and let the music play all around me.

I pick the stylus up and place it carefully onto the ancient seven inch single of "*Lions In My Own Garden*." It's the first single Prefab Sprout ever released. I can't believe that Brian has never heard of them.

"Listen to all that crackling!" Brian says.

"I like it," it's like part of the music to me. It makes it seem older, more real. It's not as if there's that much crackling on any of the records anyway. Dad must've looked after them (or hardly played them) and I make sure they never get damaged.

I don't often have people come into my house – but Brian turned up after school and it was absolutely tipping down with rain. I couldn't *not* ask him in. It's not like we're the best of friends or anything – I think his mam works and he doesn't like going home to an empty house straight after school.

My mam shot me a horrible look when I asked if Brian could come in.

"Well," she said, "I suppose he'll have to. I hope your room is tidy because he can't come in here." She meant the living room – she doesn't like strangers seeing her in the wheel-chair. It's a shame because the house is spotless. Ever since she was first diagnosed she's made it her mission to keep the house clean and tidy so that nobody thinks she can't cope. Social services tried to send round a woman two or three times a week to do that sort of stuff but mam used to dust before she even got here! And then my nanna did it all again. My nanna always says that the problem with people nowadays is that they don't do enough house-work. In her day, she tells me, people didn't have time for depression or drink because they were too busy cleaning their cupboards out. Mam isn't too happy about me going on the Geography trip, either. She thinks it's a waste of money. It *is* sixteen quid – but I did save up and pay for it myself. I even saved up some extra to pay for drinks and food and that kind of stuff. Of course, if I'm away for the weekend it means my nanna is going to have to stay. They don't get on at the best of times – and nanna will be miserable because she'll be missing the bingo. I won't be here to calm things down.

"Why would they want you to go to the Lake District?" Mam said. "It's nearly Winter. People go to the Lake District when it's sunny. It's beautiful in the Summer. You're all going to get soaked!"

"Don't you have any chart stuff?" Brian says when he's finished looking through my cassettes.

"I don't really like chart stuff," I say, which is true. "I don't listen to the radio very much because everything sounds the same. It's all young lasses and lads trying to sound American".

"Geek," says Brian, and I suppose he's right. I'd rather be a geek than a chart tart like him.

"Some of this stuff will always sound brilliant."

"It's old," Brian laughs, "I'm surprised you haven't got Frank Sinatra or Doris Day in amongst this lot." I almost tell him that I'm on the Library waiting list for the Sinatra Collection – but he'll just take the mickey.

"Prefab Sprout came from round here," I tell him, "well, from County Durham anyway."

"I've never heard of them."

"You should give them a try – they do proper songs – they're quite funny, too".

"No thanks," he says, "I'm still recovering from when you lent me that Morrissey tape you kept going on about – you said *that* was funny but it made me want to slash my wrists."

I found out today that Nikki likes Morrissey. Actually – that was the best bit of the whole day. I thought Tuesday was going to be dull because Nikki and I don't have any of the same lessons. We're in different groups for stuff like Maths and Science. Apart from English, where I'm in the top set, I'm in the middle groups for most subjects. It's not like I'm thick, I just don't like wasting my time on homework for something like maths. What's the point since calculators can do it all for you? At least in English there's more than one way to be right about something. My brother was in top set for everything, and maybe that was important to him. My mam used to always go on about it.   Anyway,   Nikki waved at me across the dining hall – I usually sit on my own eating my sandwiches and doing homework so that I don't have to do it at home, but not today. She didn't seem self-conscious at all. She yelled "Chris!" right across the dining hall – and everyone turned around to look in my direction. I must've gone completely scarlet. I was amazed for lots of reasons. She's only new to the school and she acts as if she owns the place – and also, *nobody* ever calls to me like that – especially not girls.

Nikki hurried over and squeezed onto the bench seat next to me.

"You OK?"

"Not bad," I said, absolutely amazed that she'd come looking for me to sit next to. I didn't eat anything else. I had visions of choking on the corned beef in my sarnie while talking to Nikki. That would be awful.

"You go home the Burn way, don't you?" How does she know that? I just nodded. "I thought I saw you yesterday! Why didn't you shout and stop me?"

"I – I – didn't see you," I lied, "my eyes are bad and I only wear my glasses indoors." This is true – I've only got one pair so I can't risk them getting knackered. I'm not taking them on the Geography trip at all.

"That's mint," she says, "I'll hang on after last lesson and we can walk home the same way together!" I was so pleased I'd already decided to give up on the sandwiches.

Nikki sat and chatted to me right the way through lunch time. I can't remember much of what we talked about because I was concentrating on not saying anything stupid or boring.

She *did* wait for me after last lesson, and we did walk home together. We actually had to share my umbrella because it started raining as we walked across the school field. Nikki was amazed that I had my own umbrella.

"Well, it's not like I could rob my nanna's," I said, and Nikki laughed. I wasn't trying to be funny. My nanna doesn't have an umbrella since I bought her a rain-hat for her birthday.

We slipped and slid down the bank – together- and across the Burn bridge. I tried to start a conversation about the horrible weather and Nikki said:

"Aye, today's a real Morrissey of a day!"

"What d'you mean?"

"Bloody miserable!" She laughed.

"I think he's funny," I told her, "but nobody else seems to."

"He's hilarious," she said, "I mean, that hair!"

Before I knew it, we were outside Nikki's house – and we said all that goodbye, see you tomorrow sort of stuff. I actually felt about three feet taller walking the rest of the way on my own.

I planned to go home, sort my uniform and the dishes out and listen to some Morrissey. At last – I'd found somebody who liked something that I liked! Then Brian turned up on the door-step.

"Oh yes," he said, "I saw you walking home with the new girl!" He winked at me and elbowed me in the stomach.

Brian leaves when the rain stops.

"You should be more careful choosing your friends," Mam says, "he used this place to shelter from the rain!"

"It was pouring down, mam."

"He's a user. You don't want to be a door-mat all your life. I have and look what's happened to me!" I don't answer her. She's made her mind up.

Letter to the Prime Minister

46 Sampson Place
Newton Aycliffe
County Durham

Dear Prime Minister,

Thank you for taking the time to read this letter. Life must be pretty hectic for you, what with the elections and that war still going on, so it really is appreciated.

I've been watching the news and a lot of people are worried about Global Warming and the damage that we are doing to the environment. It is really bad and unless something gets done soon, future generations will not have such a nice place to live in. As I was watching, I had a very good idea how we could help save the planet.

I think we should ban cars from being on the road between 6am and 10am every week-day morning. Think about it. If everybody had to catch a bus or train to get to work, then the amount of pollution would be cut massively! Some people might even walk – which would make them healthier, too. I walk to school every day but I see lots of other young people being dropped off by parents – it's not doing them or the environment any good!

If people broke the law and did drive between 6 and 10, they should be put in prison for a month. I know this sounds harsh, but the planet is in such a mess that tough punishments may be the only thing that will make people stop driving their cars.

I know that cigarettes have health warnings on them – so why don't we have them on cars? I'm sure people wouldn't be so keen to drive if they had a Government Health Warning written on their bonnet. Instead of 'Smoking Kills', we could have 'Pollution Kills the Planet'. It would really make people think twice before they buy a car.

I'm sure you could try these ideas in my town. If it works it could be used everywhere within a matter of weeks! I know our Town Council would like to help as I have written to our Mayor with lots of ideas about how to improve things. It might be nice if you mention my name when you contact her.

Anyway, good luck with the election (and the war).
Yours sincerely,

Christopher Mason

Looking For Atlantis

Wednesday Morning at the Hospital

"You should've said something!" Mam glowers at me.

"What d'you mean?"

"You should have told him how bad things have been!" We're sitting in the Passenger Transport Ambulance, and it's crawling through the streets of Darlington. It stops every few feet to let people off and on. It's like the slowest bus in the world and it's for ill people. With all the coughing and sneezing that goes on, everybody will be ten times more ill after sharing each other's germs on this trip.

"You told him everything," I say, "I don't think you missed anything out."

"Yes, but that's not the point – doctors never believe what you tell them – you could've backed me up!" She tuts loudly. "He might have done more if you'd spoken up a bit."

Mam got up early this morning to do her hair and make-up. I felt like telling her she should try to look more ill when we go to the hospital, but she always behaves as if she's going to a film premiere or something. She's even wearing sun-glasses in the ambulance. She gets like this when she's going to see somebody important at the hospital. She doesn't bother dressing up for our regular doctor.

Today was the first time I'd met Mr. Harper. You could tell he was important because everybody has to call him 'Mister' rather than 'Doctor'. He wasn't wearing a tie, either. And he hadn't shaved. He seemed really nice – he looked interested in what my mam had to say and he took lots of notes. It looked to me like he believed what she was saying. When I tell my mam this, she shakes her head;

"You're too easily taken in. He's a two-faced bugger like the rest of them. He wants you to think that he cares and he makes all the right noises but he never *does* anything. He just sends me away and says 'see you in six months'."

The fact is, and mam knows this – there's nothing Mr. Harper can do. He can put her on those liquids in bags that go up the tube and into her arm and maybe some more painkillers, but at the end of the day he can't stop her from being ill. They've told us it's about *'managing the symptoms'* rather than making her better. As we sat in his office, I thought about that. As he listened and scribbled, I thought – *all three of us know that there isn't a cure and all three of us know that she's going to get worse but nobody's talking about it..*

When Harper asked us if we had any questions, I actually thought about Australia. I wanted to ask him if he thought the climate and sunshine would help with the symptoms. But all I did was shake my head. If we do get to Australia, Harper will want to know how well my mam is and then he'll write an article for one of those clever medical journals. Maybe he'll say that everyone who's ill like my mam would benefit from being in a warmer country and he'll have to tell everyone that it was my idea.

"You're like a plank of wood," mam says, "you just sit there and never say anything when I need you to!" I look out of the windows of the ambulance at all the rows of houses. Mam always says that we live in a slum, and that unless I stick in at school I'll always live in these little streets. I know she thinks I'm a lazy bugger and she's even said I should get a part-time job or a paper round. I told her that I'd asked in the shops, but they all told me I couldn't start working til I'm 16. I try to explain but she never answers – so I don't know if I ever change her mind about anything.

It's going to be another hour before we get home.

"Your dad was just the same – he always had a gob on him, mind – you could never shut him up – until you actually needed him to say something." I know mam must be cross with me, because she always compares me to my dad when I've done something to *really* upset her. "It's funny," she says, "because he's done nothing to help bring you up – but you're still a lot like him." I wonder if I should stop listening to his old records.

Mam never met anybody else after dad left so I try to help out as much as I can. I don't think I do too badly – I hoover and dust once a week but I haven't tried doing the ironing since my nanna laughed at the crease I put in my school trousers. Every Saturday morning I walk into town to get the shopping done. I bet nobody else at school does any of that stuff for their mams. When I get home from school, I empty the kitchen bin and clear away any dishes that might be on the draining board. This is before I put my school stuff away or change out of my uniform. And mam *always* insists that I change out of my uniform after school. It saves on the washing.

Apart from all that, mam seems to have forgotten that it was me who got her doctor to listen in the first place. That was an awful time. My brother said he couldn't come home because he had important exams. Mam was stuck in bed even more than usual. She just couldn't move.

"The doctors don't do home visits anymore, you'll have to bring your mum down to the surgery." I'd called our local doctor, but his receptionist was proper snotty on the phone.

"But I can't bring her down – she can't get out of bed."

"Well, what's wrong with her?" I thought this was a bloody stupid question. Why would I want a doctor if I knew what was wrong with mam? And why wasn't the receptionist more helpful? Didn't she get paid money for helping people and getting doctors to speak to patients?

"We don't know what's going on, but she's getting worse and that's why she needs a doctor!"

"But you must have some idea." I imagined this woman sitting at her desk, reading a magazine or texting someone on her mobile.

"She can't move, she says her back is hurting and she says her legs are numb. She needs help and I don't know what to do." I could feel a big lump in my throat. I wanted to swear and yell at this woman.

"Can't you get her into a taxi?" She wasn't listening, she didn't care.

"She can't move. I'm her son. I'm staying off school because I'm so worried – can I please speak to a doctor?"

The woman did eventually let me speak to a doctor, but he didn't come to see mam until after his surgery hours finished. It was after six in the evening when he showed up. I had to leave the room when he looked at her, but he called me back in so that he could talk to both of us.

"Well, Mrs. Mason, you have a trapped nerve in your back."

"Is there something she can take for it?"

"These things usually sort themselves out – but I'll make sure you're seen by someone at the hospital. It doesn't hurt to get it checked out."

"Is there a prescription I can get for her?" The doctor carried on talking to me and mam, but didn't look me in the eye or answer any of my questions.

Mam had to stay in bed for nearly a month before her appointment came through at the hospital. She only got it that soon because my nanna paid for her to go private. That was when nanna first had to come and stay with us. That month was the worst. It was when we didn't know what was really wrong and the doctor wouldn't give her any tablets or anything until she'd been to the hospital. And my nanna sat around tutting a lot. I don't think she believed there was anything wrong with mam.

Looking For Atlantis

When mam did see the specialist he wanted to keep her in for tests. She had to have steroids pumped into her. Me and nanna had to trail through on the bus every day to visit her. I missed a lot of school. My nanna didn't say very much about what was going on. We'd sit on the bus and she'd talk about the weather and the names of the pubs we passed and the funny road signs for places like 'Pityme' and 'Shincliffe' but she never explained what was happening at the hospital. I know that the specialist spoke to her about mam, but none of that information got passed on to me. I suppose she thought I was too young to know what was going on. I was imagining all sorts. I'd heard my nanna telling my brother all about it on the phone but she did that quiet grown up talking so I couldn't hear what was happening. I thought it was a bit daft. I mean, I was the one that lived with mam all the time, and I did most of the stuff like ringing doctors and making sure she took her tablets, but I was the one who didn't know what was going on!

Then mam came home and the council came round to put in a stair-lift and a ramp and handles in the bath-rooms. Mam was given walking sticks and a wheel-chair. All the time the council people were at our house my mam just sat there without saying anything. I had to let them in and deal with them and thank them because my mam didn't even look at them.

To begin with, mam used to come out with into town now and again. We'd walk to the shops and I'd push her in the chair. I know she didn't like being seen in a wheel-chair but she seemed to be getting used to it. But then funny things started to happen. I first noticed it when we were in the bakery. If I was standing behind mam, the people behind the counter would speak to me, and ask me what I wanted. They never spoke to mam. Even after she'd given them money to pay for what we'd bought, they'd hand the change to me. I expected my mam to say something sarcastic to the people who ignored her – she'd always been sarcastic at home – but it was like she was slowly disappearing and she wasn't doing a thing to stop it.

She stopped going out to the shops. She told my nanna that she thought I was embarrassed being seen out with '*a cripple*' and that it wasn't right for a lad of my age to be pushing her around the shops in a wheel-chair. I couldn't have cared less what people thought. She was still my mam and I was doing my best to make sure she still got out and about. My mam used *me* as an excuse to stop leaving the house. She said that she wanted me to have a normal life. I don't know what that means. What is a normal life? She said that she wants me to go to University and get out of this town, but I don't know if I want to go – it sounds like it costs a lot of money and we never see my brother because he has to work so hard. And my school work takes a bit of a back seat nowadays so I don't know if they'll even let me do A levels, never mind anything after that. But mam expects me to go now that my brother has.

She's making me go into school this afternoon – even though I've only got PSHE and P.E. I've told her that both of those subjects don't really matter because we don't get exams in them, but she won't have it.

I suppose I'll get to walk home with Nikki again, though.

Reply from the Mayor Number 1

The Office of the Lord Mayor
Town Hall Chambers
21 – 25 Heighington Street

Dear Christopher,

Thank you very much for your letter. I have looked at your suggestions with a great deal of interest, and I will make sure that they are discussed at the next full meeting of the town council.

Yours sincerely

Theresa Rutter (Mrs.)

Letter to the Mayor Number 2

46 Sampson Place
Newton Aycliffe
County Durham

Dear Mrs. Rutter,

Hi! I've just seen your picture in our free paper and I have to say you like very dignified wearing your chains and hat. You were in a photograph opening the new community centre and there were loads of young people smiling in the picture with you. It's obvious that you have taken a big interest in the young people in our town and I think that's brilliant! As a young person myself, I'm also interested in what happens to them.

Some of the young people in our town get into the local newspaper for the wrong reasons, don't they? Like when they've been causing trouble in the town centre. There have been stories about shop lifting, fighting and some of them have even been threatening to push old people in front of cars! I've seen for myself how young people gather on a Saturday afternoon and make life miserable for everyone else.

I'm sure lots of people would like to see them locked up and punished – somebody on the news even suggested that there should be a curfew! It would have to be a pretty early curfew to stop them hanging around the shops at 2 o'clock on a Saturday afternoon.

Anyway; I've got some ideas that would make life better for everyone. First of all, I think the Leisure Centre in our town needs to be improved. At the moment there is a swimming pool that nobody uses because it looks dirty, and there are some squash courts but no squash equipment. I don't know how much it would cost to sort these things out, but I do think it would be worth it. Some people hang around because they haven't got anything to do – so they need somewhere to go. Our town isn't big enough to have a cinema or a bowling alley – so we need things like the swimming pool to be a better place to go.

I think we should also let young people use the Leisure Centre for free at the weekends. It would encourage them to stay off the streets and also to get healthy (which is a big thing in the news at the moment). I know it sounds mad to spend money doing up the Leisure Centre and then giving stuff away for free, but I do have a plan to make it work. In order to use the swimming pool or squash courts for free, young people would have to agree to spend an hour picking up litter in the town centre on Saturday morning. I'm sure you'll agree that this is a simple but brilliant idea. The town centre will be tidier, the young people will be helping the community, and they will have somewhere to go to get some exercise! They might also start to appreciate that hard work earns rewards!

I think it would be good for the town, and it's a way of rewarding people instead of punishing them.

Let me know what you think!

Yours sincerely,

Christopher Mason

Wednesday Afternoon at School

"Bloody hell." You can hear just about everybody swearing as we line up for cross country. By this time of the year, the school field is like a swamp. They don't bother playing football on it any more, it's just the starting point for two miles of muddy stupidity. The teachers seem to take a sick pleasure in making us do cross country in the half-term before Christmas. I don't know why they can't let us do it in the Summer – it would make quite a pleasant walk at that time of year.

We've just been watching one of those 'relationship' videos in PSHE. It was terrible. The actors were supposed to be teenagers but they looked about thirty and they kept using words that they think kids use like '*wicked*', '*safe*' and '*bonus*.' After thirty five minutes of them sitting around and getting a bit angry with each other, we found out that people need to speak to each other more. The teacher (Mrs Clarkson) actually handed out work sheets telling us how important it is to let people know how you feel. It was well worth coming into school for *that*. I wonder what would have happened if I'd told her I felt bored and utterly patronised after her lesson. I bet she'd think twice about encouraging us to express our feelings in future. The lesson was even worse because they always put us in groups of boys and girls for PSHE in case anybody gets embarrassed. I haven't seen Nikki at all today so far. And now I've got to put up with Mr. Parr.

Apart from the mud and the rain, the worst thing about cross country is the fact that the sporty kids like Adrian Wilson and Anthony Gray can run the whole thing in eleven or twelve minutes. My best ever time is just under nineteen minutes and Mr. Parr always writes our names and times on a wall-chart in the P.E. block. I always have the slowest times in our year group. Maybe it's because of all the chocolate biscuits that me and mam get through on a weekend. I get made to feel like a freak because Mr. Parr tells me to set off a couple of minutes before everyone else. He says that he's trying to make it fair by giving me a head-start, but I just think he likes to make everyone watch me as I struggle to run across the field towards the Burn path. The school P.E. kit doesn't help. I'm still wearing last years', so my bottle green top is too tight around my stomach. My arms and legs are pretty skinny but my belly looks massive – to the rest of the kids I must look like a lumpy apple on pipe-cleaners.

"Off you go, Mason," he shouts and blows his whistle. There's a fine rain stinging my legs and face as I huff and puff across the field. I don't get far before I can feel the air burning in my nostrils and throat. I have a stitch. I try to breathe through my nose because somebody told me that it helps, but it just seems to make things worse. Mud starts to splash up onto my socks and legs. It's cold and slimy and my feet stick to the gloopy ground.

I'm knackered by the time I reach the fence and leave the school field. I hit the Burn path, slowing to a walk. The studs on my football boots scrape on the concrete. I should really try walking on the grass, but I'm already covered in mud and my mam will go mad.

I haven't gotten very far along the path that leads down towards the Burn before people start overtaking me. Adrian Wilson is first. He doesn't say anything, he just breezes past – all long arms and legs and speed..

"You're supposed to run, Mason!" Mr. Parr is yelling at me. He follows the runners from the top of the bank at the edges of the school field. P.E. teachers always call people by their second names. I don't know why that is. It's like they want to think they're in the army and tougher than they really are. Some of the kids reckon that Mr. Parr used to be a Prison Warder. I can well believe it. He has a thick, low fore-head and a prominent chin – his nick-name has always been '*monkey*' or '*gibbon*' – but I can think of much worse things to call him. "Run! It's called a cross country *run!*"

I'm out of breath. I've got a stitch. I'm not running because I don't think I can. Mr. Parr shouts something else at me, but I can't make it out. He's off back across the school field, probably so he can watch the rest of the kids as they overtake me and head towards the Burn bridge. When we reach the bridge we're supposed to turn around and come back, but Parr probably thinks everyone stops for a ciggie or a drink.

If the weather was half-decent this would be OK. I don't suppose they have this problem in Australia. I remember seeing one of those Christmas programmes where they use a satellite link to let people speak to their relatives on the other side of the world – and Australia had bright sunshine in December! I wonder if my cousins have to do cross country. At least they won't get dead muddy.

Going for a walk down The Burn can be quite nice when it gets overgrown and the council don't bother cutting it back, but the track has been made wider and filthier by the heavy footprints of the runners. I carefully pick my way through grassier patches. The rain has made everything look greener and fresher – but it's also made the ground sloppier and stickier. I stop and pick twigs and branches from trees, bending and twisting them as I stroll through this little bit of wilderness. I could quite happily stay out here all afternoon.

"Still walking, eh?" Adrian Wilson passes me for the second time. He's on his way back already. He must be trying to break his own record. He is covered in long splashes of muck. He doesn't care. A load of kids follow not far behind him – some of them are really pushing themselves. They've got red faces and are panting like dogs. Maybe they don't realise just how pointless this whole cross country crap is. I mean – what's the point? If you're going to go out and about, surely you should stop and have a look at what's around you – even for just a few minutes?

I finally make it to the Burn bridge. The ground is really chopped up, with large pools of filthy rain-water collecting in the foot-prints. I know that Mr. Parr will already be back at the starting line, giving the kids their times, so I don't actually go right the way up to the bridge. It's not as if it's going to make a vast difference to my time. So I just turn around and start heading back the way I came. Nobody's around to call me a cheat.

I'm almost back onto the Burn path when I see three or four of the other kids throwing mud at each other. They're actually scooping it up with their bare hands and slapping it over each other's heads. Daft sods.

"Ow, Mason!" I recognise Jack 'Olly' Alton underneath his thick coating of mud. He throws a handful at me, so I step out of the way. My legs get splattered. Olly laughs.

"Oh... piss off," I try to shout at him, to show I'm angry, but I don't shout too loudly in case he thinks I want a fight. Olly laughs even harder when the other kids join in and start chucking mud at me. In the end, I stop trying to get out the way. My attempts to dodge their missiles just makes them laugh more, so I stand there, letting them plaster my hair, my face, my shoulders, my stomach, my arms... I look like I've crawled out of the Burn. They eventually run off, still laughing. I carry on walking.

As I hit the school field, I can see Mr. Parr waiting for me. He looks from his stop-watch to me as I approach. I can feel mud hardening in my hair and I wipe my eyes and nose on my sleeve so that Parr can't see that I've been crying.

"*RUN!*" He yells. "I've got better things to do with my time!" I ignore him and continue to trudge across the school field. Maybe I should just go home. It's not that far to walk. I should walk home and tell my mam what happened. She hates Mr. Parr. "You're a complete waste of space." Parr holds up his stop-watch as I pass him. "I turned this off when it went over twenty-five minutes," he says, as if I should care about that. "Look at the state of you. I suppose you've been fighting, haven't you, in the mud?" I don't answer him. I don't even look at him. I don't want him to know that I've been crying. "You're a disgrace. Just like your brother – he thought he was too good for exercise as well. You stupid lump." I walk past him. I don't listen to what he says next. I hear him getting angrier and angrier but I just walk past him and back into the changing rooms. I wish he'd join the army and speak to people like he speaks to me. They might shoot him in the head or reverse a tank over him.

Mr. Parr has always had it in for me, ever since mam rang him up when my brother was in the first year of Comprehensive. Back then, we still had the phone on, and mam used to like using it to argue with people. Parr had given my brother a lousy report after his first full term at the school – he said he was lazy, lacked motivation, and needed to take more exercise. My mam was furious. She rang him up and told him about how intelligent and hard working my brother is and about how he shouldn't have to do P.E. because he has brains.

"He's overweight," Parr had said, "he needs to get more fresh air and exercise. He's a useless lump."

"How dare you!" Mam had really shouted at him. "It's no wonder the kids call you a bloody monkey!"

Mr. Parr had put the phone down on her.

****
****

"Well, well, well..." Mrs. Nixon waddles into her office. She's scowling as usual. "It seems we aren't so perfect after all!" She sounds happy. She really sounds like she's glad I'm in trouble. She must've been waiting for this since I first started at school. It doesn't help that I still have dried streaks of mud on my face and in my hair – Mr. Parr wouldn't let me take a shower - he wanted me to get dressed and come straight to Mrs. Nixon's office.

"This will have to go down on your permanent record!" She talks like she's got squishy toffee or a great big wedge of peanut butter stuck to the back of her teeth - and you can always see spit collecting at the corners of her mouth. Her eyes are sparkly. "Stand up straight when I'm talking to you," she hisses, "and tuck that shirt in – I've never seen anything like it." Somebody really needs to point out just how untidy she looks. She's like a knackered old settee – all her lumps and bumps are in the wrong places. Now probably isn't a good time for me to tell her that.

"I should call your mother," she clucks, but I don't bother to tell her that we haven't got the phone on at the moment. "I always knew you were trouble," she stares at me with beady little eyes, "your brother never got sent to me – not for fighting, anyway. It used to be a pleasure seeing him – he was always getting merits and coming top in his exams. It seems that lightning didn't strike your family twice though did it?" I don't know why she hates me. I've only ever been good at school. I've never been late, I'm only off when mam is really poorly, I'm never any bother for the teachers and I always try my best! What does she want? "Mr. Parr says you've always been a problem in P.E."

"I always try my best," I blurt out, "it's not my fault if I can't run fast."

"DON'T BACK ANSWER ME!" I've just given her the excuse she needed to scream right in my face. White spit lands on my jacket. "I AM TALKING!" She looks like one of them rubber Halloween masks, all big nostrils and mad staring eyes. "YOU MUST THINK YOU'RE SO MUCH BETTER THAN ANYONE ELSE BECAUSE YOUR BROTHER GOT FIVE 'A's FOR HIS A-LEVELS! WELL LET ME TELL YOU…" She pauses briefly, winding herself up for another machine gun burst. "…THAT'S NOT YOU!!! I'VE SEEN BRIGHTER, MUCH BRIGHTER, PUPILS

THAN YOU, END UP IN DEAD END JOBS – AND DO YOU KNOW WHY?" I'm not sure if she expects me to speak or if that would just make things even worse. I shake my head pathetically. "BECAUSE YOUR ATTITUDE STINKS! YOU THINK YOU'RE TOO GOOD TO DO AS YOU'RE TOLD – AND THAT WON'T WASH IN THE WORLD OF WORK!!!!"

Her face is now bright purple, she really should sit down and have a drink of water or something. She is getting on a bit. "WHAT HAVE YOU GOT TO SAY FOR YOURSELF?"

"Sorry?" I don't mean for it to sound like a question, but I don't think any answer is going to be taken very well by this woman.

"AND YOU'D BETTER MEAN IT!" All of a sudden her voice drops to a whisper; "In a couple of years time, someone is going to write to me – it will be an employer or if you're very very very lucky, a University – and they'll ask me to give them a reference – to tell them all about you. And do you know what? I'm not sure what sort of reference I'm going to give – not after today's little performance. I'm going to be watching you Christopher Mason – I'm going to be watching you like a hawk."

Sometimes I almost feel sorry for her. The kids call her *Hopalong* or *Peg* because she walks with a limp. Once, in assembly, she told us about how she'd had Polio as a child. She was stuck in bed for months and she hasn't been able to walk properly. I thought it was a funny thing to tell kids in an assembly. It was almost as if she knew about her nick-name and wanted us to feel horrible. Sometimes I've thought about going to see her and telling her about my mam and how she can't walk at all because she's so ill. She'd probably just think I was being cheeky and yell at me some more.

Nikki is waiting for me when I'm eventually allowed to leave. She must be able to read my thoughts because the first thing she says is;

"Life's not fair is it?"

"So you heard about it, then?"

"Pretty much the whole of our year-group heard Nixon yelling – and if it means anything, most people couldn't believe that it was you getting all the grief."

"She's nuts," I say, "she really is nuts. She didn't let me explain anything – she just threatened me with permanent records and references and stuff."

"Ah, I wouldn't worry about," Nikki shrugs, "it's not like you were gonna get a brilliant report in P.E. anyway." I wonder how Nikki knows about me and P.E. It must be common knowledge, I suppose, especially in our year group. It doesn't matter – I'm just made up that she waited for me after school.

A Happy Ending

"It was all just a stupid mistake." That's what he says. The man has made bacon sandwiches and he sits and explains as Chris eats. They are in a large, bright kitchen, sitting at an enormous antique dining table. The room is heated by one of those old antique stoves and fresh vegetables hang from a ceiling rack. Chris feels instantly at home, even though he's never been here before in his life.

"We were too young," he goes on, in between mouthfuls of bacon and bap, "it certainly wasn't your fault that we split up." Chris beams as he hears this. "Sometimes two people just can't live together, it's nobody's fault it's just how things are."

Chris' latest school report lies open on the table. All of the teachers have been nice about him – apart from the monkey faced P.E. Teacher, but Chris had been expecting that.

"You've done really well, Chris. I'm very proud of you. Despite all of the upset and worries that you've had, you've made me so proud of you. You've shown everybody just how smart and hard-working you are." Chris is embarrassed. He's too modest to take compliments like this.

"Your Mam and I were stupid and selfish," the man says. "We put ourselves first – and we didn't realise that when you have children, you always have to put them before anything else. We had our disagreements but we shouldn't have gotten you involved. I only wish I could turn the clock back." He looks down and for a moment they sit in silence and think about what has been said.

"I thought about you every day," he goes on, "every day since I left. I used to sit and cry at Christmas and on your Birthday. I used to cry and wish I could be with you. I felt like my life was over. It was only because of my new religious beliefs that I couldn't send you cards or presents."

"That's OK, I understand," says Chris, "Mam always used to say that you didn't care or that you'd forgotten about me, but I always knew there must be some reason why you didn't get in touch."

"I just want to be part of your life." The man's eyes fill with tears. "I know I've let you down and I'm so very sorry. I'll make it all up to you, even if it takes me the rest of my life. I know a couple of blokes who work as bouncers – they'll have a quiet word with that P.E. Teacher and make sure he doesn't hassle you anymore... and then there's this..." He slides an envelope across the table. Chris opens it carefully. Two return tickets. Australia.

"Thank you." Now Chris can feel tears in his own eyes. He swallows. "Thank you, thank you...."

No. I can't do it. It doesn't work.
I can't call him Dad – not even in a daydream.

Wednesday after School

"Aww – look at the Queen." My Nanna peers over her glasses at the TV. She takes another mouthful of tea. "Sssslurp-gulp-aaaaaah!" Nanna doesn't really watch or listen to much telly, but she does talk over the top of programmes if other people are watching it.

"Why," I say, "what's wrong with the Queen?"

"She's got so many worries," my nanna says – as if it's the most obvious thing in the world. "Nearly all of her children have been divorced and it's awful to see your bairns go through that."

"Loads of people have to put up with that. Nearly half of all marriages end in divorce." Mr. McPherson told us that in Geography. I can't remember what it had to do with the lesson but I thought it was quite an interesting point. It made me feel better about mam and dad not being together any more. There must be millions of kids like me all over the world. I wonder if they're all as fed up as I am?

"And she always has to keep a stiff upper lip," my nanna went on, "the Queen can't moan or whinge about her problems, she just has to get on with it."

"What does she have to get on with?" My nanna has always loved the Queen. I don't know why. "She spends all of her life on holiday. She has loads of people working for her – I bet she doesn't even have to choose her own hats or wipe her own bum."

"You should have more respect for your elders and betters." I never know if my Nanna is winding me up when she says stuff like this. "You shouldn't be jealous of privileged people – you have to know your place."

"I'm not jealous." I don't think I am. I don't want to be Queen. "But what does the Queen do?" I say. And I mean it. "It's not like she's got a job. She doesn't even rule the country like the Kings and Queens used to."

"We'd all be better off if she did," nanna says, "she'd take us back to the old fashioned values." I haven't got a clue what she means by this. My nanna always talks about the past being better than the present – but if the old songs she sings (usually while she's washing the dishes) are anything to by then I'm not so sure. "Old people never used to worry about being out after dark, and you could leave your back door unlocked all night... People prefer a strong leader."

"Next you'll be saying we should have had Hitler in charge!"

"Don't be so stupid. Your Grandad was in the war." She doesn't mention him very often. She's been a widow since she was thirty-nine. Mam says she wore black every day for a year after he died. But she never cried or said anything about it. I've always wanted to ask my nanna about my Grand-father but I don't want to upset her. I know they met during the War and that he was in the air-force, and I know that he died when my mam was very little but that's about it. My mam says that when she was little they were so poor that they couldn't even have a head-stone for her dad – so he's buried in a cemetery and nobody even knows which grave is his. I decide to change the subject.

"Have you heard anything from Auntie Pat lately?" Nanna normally tells us if she's had a letter from Australia. She only gets her post when she goes home at a weekend.

"Not since my Birthday," that was five months ago, "she always puts a long letter in with the card – I suppose it saves on the postage." My nanna approves of stuff like that. I mean – why pay for two envelopes? It doesn't matter that people might appreciate the thought – not when there's a few pence to be saved. "Your cousins are both doing well in school and your Uncle Pete has been made an executive at the company that he works for." She doesn't seem to think it's strange that she hasn't heard anything from them for nearly half a year.

"My mam never hears from them."

"She got a Christmas card – I remember seeing it. Didn't she put a letter in with that?"

"I don't think so." I don't remember seeing one. She only ever writes '*with love from Pat and family*' in our Christmas card. It's not a personal message at all.

"Well, they lead very busy lives out there – Pat works in a bank and they both joined a tennis club. It's supposed to be a lovely life out there!"

"Hmmm." I think about all of this. If the last thing mam heard from Pat was at Christmas, then they never bothered with either of our birthdays. "Mam always wanted to go and visit them out there."

"I've never heard her say that."

"She did. She said Auntie Pat told her she'd be welcome any time." Nanna doesn't say anything – she just does her 'sucked-lemon' face again. "It might be a good idea – the warm and the sun might make mam feel better."

"It's costs a bally fortune to go over there! It's the other side of the world!"

"It'd be worth it, if it made mam feel better. Auntie Pat did say…"

"Yes, and she asked me to go over as well, but it costs too much money and they're always very – they do a lot of entertaining – and your cousins both go to private schools. They've got all kinds of expenses."

"I thought Auntie Pat and Uncle Pete might want to help mam out. We *are* family, after all. You've just said he's an executive and Pat works at a bank. They could help us out. I could even pay them back when I'm older and I've got a job."

"You've got a lot to learn about the world, our Chris," she says, looking over her glasses at me, "they've earned what they've got – and they've worked bally hard for it. It's not their fault that your mam isn't well."

"I'm not saying that it's their fault, I just thought they might want to help."

Looking For Atlantis

We sit in silence for a bit. I can tell she doesn't want to talk about Auntie Pat or Australia or anything like that. Nanna drinks more of her tea. I do too. It's lukewarm and I think about putting the kettle on again. From being very small, I've always drank more tea than coke or pop. I know this might be a bit strange for someone of my age (and some of the kids at school do think I'm a bit of a freak) but I really would rather have tea. My nanna has tried to teach me the art of perfect tea making, and there's always a constant demand for the stuff in this house.

"What's better than a nice cup of tea?" my nanna says. "Two cups of tea!" Then she laughs and nods and *I* have to go and put the kettle on. Again. She also does this weird thing when she drinks – she slurps her tea loudly, then makes a horrible swallowing noise before letting out a loud sigh. It sort of goes ssssslurp-gulp-aaaaaah! And she does it every time she has a sip of tea. Ssssslurp-gulp-aaaaaah! She does it a lot. In the morning, I always take mam a cup of tea up to her room.

"Eeh," nanna suddenly says, breaking the long lull, "if I was at home I could've been at Hagan Hall!" Nanna also loves bingo. Before mam got ill and nanna had to spend most of the week at our house, she used to go to a different bingo hall every night of the week. When I was younger she used to take me with her as a lucky mascot. The old people didn't seem to mind at first, but then my nanna started buying me my own bingo cards. After I won a pound for a full house, the woman that ran the bingo told my nanna that she couldn't bring me anymore – it was illegal to let a child play bingo. And one of the other old women said it was a disgrace that "bloody kids are allowed to come and take money off poor old pensioners!" They didn't seem to mind when I wasn't winning.

"Do you think the queen goes to bingo?" I ask.

"I bet she'd like to – probably too busy."

"That makes two of you, then."

"Put the kettle on will you, Chris?"

Mark Magrs

Letter to the Prince of Wales

46 Sampson Place
Newton Aycliffe
County Durham

Dear Charles,

I hope you and your family are keeping well. My mam hasn't been so well recently, but we're getting by because my nanna comes and helps out. It must be great having a big family like yours. Everybody probably helps out when someone isn't well.

I've been watching the news about the refugee crisis in the middle-east and I think it's awful. They had an appeal on the telly asking for money and they showed pictures of children who have been shot or blown up.

I only get £2 a week pocket money because my dad doesn't live with us anymore – but this week I gave it all to the refugee appeal. I read in the paper that your mam is the second richest woman in the country, and I thought since you probably get your money from her, it might be a good idea if you gave one week of your money to the refugee appeal. It would be great if you went on the telly and told everybody how much you were giving to help the refugee crisis – I'm sure it would set a brilliant example and mean that lots more people would dig in to their pockets. People like my nanna always say that 'charity begins at home' so they don't want to help people in other countries – but my nanna is a big fan of the Royal Family so if you told her to help I'm sure she would.

Between you and your family, you could probably send some money to the starving people in Africa, too! Everything helps!

Looking For Atlantis

    Anyway, I must go as I have Graphics homework to do for tomorrow morning.
    Yours sincerely,

Christopher Mason

PS: Please tell your Mam I was asking after her.

Thursday Morning

"Everything you do looks the same, lad. Do you even bother listening to anything I tell you?" Art should be the best lesson in the world. I mean, you get to use your imagination, there aren't any boring books, and you can pretty much do what you want. Not with Mr. Mowatt.

Usually, we walk into Mr. Mowatt's classroom and he has a '*still-life*' set up. It's always a vase with some dried flowers, or a tea-pot with some fruit next to it. It's possibly the most boring thing I've ever seen, and I've watched a lot of Sunday night telly with my mam. Everybody sits and draws the flowers and tea-pots for a couple of lessons – then we either have to paint it, or design a little pot using the still-life as a starting point. I'm really not bothered about making pots, but Mr. Mowatt has a big kiln in his classroom so we're encouraged to use clay as much as possible. He's always telling us to think of things in '*three dimensions*'. He runs an after-school craft class for grown-ups on Mondays. He actually charges people to come in and do the sort of crap that we do with him for free. He must teach his adult learners how to make little clay dragons, because his kiln is always full of the buggers.

"Scruffy git never washes his clothes," Brian reckons, "he's been wearing the same green cords since we were in the first year. He only likes getting the clay out so that he's got an excuse for looking so hacky." Mr. Mowatt always wears the same jumper, too – it's an old brown and grey thing that Brian says has twenty year old lumps of clay stuck to it. "He wore that jumper when my dad came to this school." Brian is always saying he wants to leave air bubbles in one of his clay pots before it goes in the kiln because that would blow up everything that was in there at the same time. He also calls Mowatt 'egg-slicer' because he has one of those funny hairstyles – the middle of his head is completely bald so he combs bits that grow above his ears over the top. If he's on yard duty on a windy day it flips open like a lid.

"Anyway," I say to Brian, "I'm going down town after school, what sort of stuff are we supposed to be getting for the weekend?" Me and Brian and David are clubbing together to buy food supplies for the Geography trip.

"I reckon we should have a full-on fry up." Brian says his older brother has a card for the cash and carry, so he can get a load of stuff for cheaper than it is in the shops. "Bacon, fried eggs, sausages, tomatoes – you can't whack a good fry up." I'm not sure. I don't like being around hot frying pans and I'm pretty sure I'd mess something like that up.

"I dunno."

"Oh come on, I do them all the time. It's the best thing to get you warmed up." The only things we've done in food technology have been cakes and bread and butter pudding. Everything we make in the cookery rooms always seems to taste of flour and charcoal.

"We could just take some bread and ham to make sarnies."

"Sarnies? Bollocks. I'm not living off sarnies for a weekend. And we'll need something hot if they're gonna be dragging us off up mountains all weekend." I only ever have tea and toast for breakfast at home. I make my own sarnies for lunch – and on a Sunday I put one of those rolled roasts in the oven for two hours (if I've remembered to take it out of the freezer on Saturday night!) and I might do some oven chips to go with it. If we stick to sarnies at the weekend then I won't look daft – even I can make sarnies.

I wonder if Brian really can cook like he says he can. He's certainly put a lot of weight on recently. He used to go swimming every morning before school – and people used to say that he might go to the Olympics in a few years time, but then something happened to his knee and he had to give it all up.

"On an evening, we could have some of those pies-in-a-tin. You slap them together with some mushy peas or bread and butter and that's a meal in itself!"

"I suppose so…"

"Or we could get some ready made frozen lasagnes. They're all right with some bread and butter and ketchup. More of a snack than a meal, though. Anyway – leave it to me – you can always help out with the washing up…" I hope this trip is going to be OK.

"Hoi lad!" Mowatt is standing in the doorway. "Are you actually going to get something done today? Do you think this lesson is a joke, lad?" Brian and I get this lecture every few weeks. Mowatt thinks we shouldn't be able to talk in his lessons. The fact is, his idea of Art is so boring we have to keep talking just to stay awake.

One time, I decided I'd had enough of still-lifes and clay, so I brought some of my cartoons in to show him. I thought if I could show him that I was really interested and had been working in my own time then he might let me do more of what I want.

"Where did you trace these from?" He said with a grin. I told him I hadn't – I told him that I'd done them at home, all by myself. He just shrugged and snorted. "It's the sort of thing you might get away with in graphics or design, but you need to show that you can master the basics."

In our art lessons the basics are very basic. We have to do stuff in the style of Mr. Mowatt. If he likes you, then he finishes your work off for you so that it looks like something *he's* done. If he doesn't like you he just snorts and calls you *'bone idle'*.

I can kind of understand why Mowatt doesn't like Brian. Brian shouts *'comb-over'* and *'baldy'* at him in the corridor – but I always turn up on time, I always bring my own pencils and I always try my hardest even if the work is just some stupid still life. But Mowatt talks to me as though I'm useless. I think he was a bit jealous of my cartoons. He's not allowed to do stuff like that at school. He seemed to think I was big headed for bringing them in. I don't know why some teachers like putting people down. Maybe it makes them feel better or more important or something.

Funnily enough, Nikki seems to be really good at art. Mr. Mowatt keeps telling her how well she's doing and that her work '*hangs together*' well. He says the same things to Janice, Faye and Paula all the time, too.

While he's talking to the girls, Brian manages to hit the back of Mr. Mowatt's head with a piece of dried up clay.

"Right lad, get to your head of year."

"It wasn't me," says Brian, but everybody knows who did it. Brian is sitting with a big daft grin on his face, and is looking around the room as if he's waiting for a round of applause.

"GET TO YOUR HEAD OF YEAR!" Mowatt screams at Brian. Brian shrugs and walks out of the class. As he leaves, I hear him say:

"Go and slice some eggs, baldy." Brian doesn't really care if he gets sent to Mrs. Nixon. He usually tells her to stop spitting at him.

Thursday - After School

Me and nanna have to go into into town after I come home from school. I want to get a couple of things and it turns out that we don't have much milk left. My nanna doesn't have milk in her tea, so her cup always looks like it's full of hot vinegar, but mam and I need some. By the time we set off my mam gives me a list of three or four other things. She wants more chocolate biscuits.

Nanna refuses to get the bus into town. She could walk for England.   "It's a nice evening – it's the best part of the day!" It was freezing and dark. "Walking is what keeps me healthy!" It also saves about two quid on bus-fares. Since I turned fourteen and had to pay full fare, nanna has suggested we walk into town a lot more often.

The town centre isn't up to much. It was built about fifty years ago and the designers must have thought they were building a big futuristic place. There's a lot of concrete, stairs and ramps. I'm sure the walls used to be gleaming white when they'd just been painted, but nobody has taken any care of this place so everything looks dirty. People have written or cut their names onto the town's benches so often that the council haven't bothered trying to paint them or repair them. They even had to take the bins out because people were throwing fire-works in them, so rubbish just gets chucked on the pavement.

"Do you need to go anywhere but the store?" Nanna always calls the supermarket the 'store'. It must be one of those old-fashioned things.

"No," I say, which is true. I used to look at the novels in the newsagents but they got a lottery machine so the little book-case had to go. There really isn't anywhere else to go in town to buy anything.

Looking For Atlantis

There used to be quite a few clothes shops and even a little toy shop, but most of them have gone. Nowadays, we have a lot of charity and pound shops. Since Woolies closed the only bigger shop is the supermarket. Our supermarket has had lots of different names. Every few years it gets taken over and the sign changes colour, but it's still the same people working there. My mam used to stack shelves. She left after some assistant manager (who looked about twelve years old, she said) tried to tell her off in front of some of the customers. Mam has never let anyone tell her what to do – that's what she's always said, anyway. She used to speak to a couple of the other women she used to work with, but she doesn't bother with people anymore.

When I come down for mam's shopping I always try to be here for the shops opening on a Saturday morning. If I get down early enough I can get in and out quickly and be home before half past nine. The only other time I'll come down is if I have nanna with me. I know it sounds soft, but I don't like being in the town centre on my own. Loads of the older kids from school hang around on an afternoon – especially on a Saturday – and I don't want to be anywhere near them. I even try to avoid the younger ones because some of them try to look tough by picking on older kids. About two years ago some of them stopped me and asked what I was doing and when I told them they laughed. They laughed at the old shopping trolley that I was using (it belonged to my nanna and it really was a big help when I had a lot of shopping to carry) and tried to take it off me. They said they wanted a turn of it. I don't know what they meant by that. Did they want to do some shopping with it? Did they want to sit on it like it was a go-kart? I didn't see how it could be any use to them so they were probably planning to be mean. I ran away. Well, I tried to run, pulling the trolley behind me. They didn't chase after me but I kept trying to run anyway. I imagined them laughing at me, and planning to get me the following Saturday at the same time. When I got home I cried. I don't know why. I didn't let mam see how upset I was, I just made sure I always went into town very early on a Saturday morning from then on.

The only real problem about being in town with my nanna is the fact that she doesn't like me buying the Big Issue off the homeless guy outside of the closed-down Woolworths.

"He probably just spends all his bally money on cider or cigarettes!"

"It's probably all he has to warm himself up." I don't care what he spends his money on – if I didn't have a home I'd probably want to be drunk all the time, too. I always try to buy a Big Issue when I can afford it. He seems like quite a decent bloke – and he's never been drunk when I've spoken to him. He doesn't smell of apples so I don't know why my nanna thinks he likes cider. I do know he's called Tony, because it says so on his Big Issue seller's badge. His I.D. picture makes me feel sad because he looks so different on it. On his badge, he has a much rounder face, and his hair is longer. And he's smiling.

"How are you, mate?" He remembers me, like he always does, and he asks after my mam.

"I'm OK – how are you keeping?" I feel strange asking him how he is. I mean, he's obviously not having a brilliant time, but it seems like the right sort of thing to say.

"Not bad, not bad, this weather doesn't half take it out of you, doesn't it?" We talk about the weather like normal people are supposed to, and I give him two pounds for the magazine, and when he offers me the change – like he always does - I tell him to keep it. "I appreciate it, mate." His clothes are dark and worn out – I wonder how long he's had to wear them for. He's sometimes on crutches and he's told me that he has sores on his legs. I suppose that comes from sleeping on the ground in cold, wet places.

"You shouldn't encourage him," my nanna clucks as we walk on, "it's one thing giving beggars money, but if you get talking to them they might want to find out where you live!" My nanna doesn't trust most people. She spent the whole time I was talking to Tony pursing her lips and looking as if she'd just sucked a lemon. "And you were throwing your money about! He might think there's rich-pickings to be had!"

"I let him keep forty pence change," I tell her, "he's hardly going to follow us home on his crutches and murder us in our beds, is he?"

"You shouldn't encourage him," she says again, "he could be one of those blokes who pretends to be homeless just to con money out of people."

"Have you seen the state of his teeth?" If he is rich he wants to sack his dentist. "I don't think anybody would choose to live like that, nanna – his skin is practically yellow!"

"That's the drink," she tuts. My nanna doesn't drink apart from one or two glasses of sherry every Christmas. Her face always goes bright red and she starts talking about her husband.

Nanna always makes me push the trolley while she finds the things on the shopping list. I'm supposed to be getting bread buns and tomato sauce for the Geography trip. I'll have to make sure I don't mix up my change with my mam's. I don't want her to think that I'm short-changing her or keeping any money that I shouldn't.

I see Nikki walking up and down past the canned soup. I wonder if I'm imagining her. She looks lost and in a world of her own, swinging a supermarket basket and muttering to herself. I don't want her to see me with nanna. I don't want to her to ask any questions or see me out of my school uniform. My hair feels greasy after a day at school, lank and disgusting against my collar. I'm wearing my old shoes, too, the ones with the laces that don't match. I pull the trolley off towards the frozen food section. We don't need anything from over there, but I have to get some distance between me and Nikki.

Nanna catches up to me as I pretend to look at the oven chips.

"What are you doing over here? I only went to get the bally milk and when I turned around you'd disappeared!"

"I thought we needed chips," I lie, "I was just seeing if they had any offers on."

"No," she says taking out a crumpled piece of paper, "they're not on the list." Most of our shopping usually comes out of the big freezers. Mam doesn't like having fresh stuff in the house because it tires her out having to prepare it so we have a lot of pies and fish fingers and crispy pancakes.

"OK," I say, and start pushing the trolley towards the row of tills. I keep looking for Nikki, but she's nowhere to be seen. Maybe I did imagine her after all.

****
****

"There's a bus due," nanna says as we pack the last of our shopping into her trolley. She always says '*due*' as '*doo*' because she grew up in Norfolk. I used to laugh at the way she said beautiful and view but I grew out of it. For a while I felt guilty about having done it. Is it racist to take the mickey out of someone from Norfolk?

"I thought we were walking," I say, "mam didn't give me any bus fare."

"I'll get it. You've been at school all day. We'll be home a lot faster on the bus." This isn't really true. The town buses go round all the estates before they get to ours. They only run one bus an hour so it stops *everywhere*.

"Oh, thanks." I wonder if something's wrong with her. Maybe she needs a new hip like lots of old people do.

Looking For Atlantis

The buses are never on time, either. Eventually we manage to stack our shopping into the luggage rack of the little mini-bus. That's when I notice Nikki sitting on the bus. She's on her own and she smiles at me. I'm with my nanna. I can't go and sit near Nikki because my nanna will think that it's weird and I'll never hear the end of it. I wave at Nikki, say '*hi*', and sit down next to nanna.

Nikki appears in the seat behind us. She's moved to be nearer to us - *nearer to me*. I'm not wearing my school uniform anymore, so I'm pleased I'm sitting down. My jeans are very dodgy and slightly too small for me. I'm also wearing my bad weather coat from last year, so the sleeves are a bit frayed and it really could do with a wash.

"Y'all right Chris?"

"I'm fine – how are you?"

"Oh you know – just picking up some supplies for the weekend!" Nikki hold up her shopping bags – they're full of crisps, sweets and cans of tomato soup.

"Yeah – I had to get some too!" I don't show her the bread-buns and tomato sauce. My nanna coughs. It's not a real cough.

"Aren't you going to introduce me to your friend?"

"Erm, yes, this is Nikki from school…"

"Nice to meet you!" Nikki nods at nanna

"…and this is my *grand-mother*."

"*Grand-mother*?" Nanna does her sucked lemon face. "That makes me sound so old! I'm his nanna! He never calls me grand-mother!" Nikki laughs. I cringe.

"You looking forward to the trip?"

"I dunno," I say, "Brian said he wants to do all the cooking."

"Bloody hell!" She giggles. "He's a nut-case! Did you see what he did to Mowatt this morning?" Nanna turns her nose up at the language Nikki uses.

"Yeah," I reply, "everybody always knows it's him that does stuff like that – he can't help looking guilty."

I suddenly realise that Nikki will be getting off the bus *after* we do. She's going to see where I live. She's going to see the street that I live on. She's going to know that I live in the council houses, and people always think the worst if they know you live in a council house. They all think we have scary dogs and beat each other up all the time. If I was on my own I could stay on the bus past my stop and pretend that I live somewhere nice.

"Press the bell," nanna says, so I do. The bus starts to slow down. I look out of the window, and I can see the woman next door smacking her two-year old round the head as she tries to get him back into the house. Bloody hell.

"Well, our stop," I try to smile at Nikki.

"Yes," she says, "see you in the morning!" This is the worst bit. Not only am I getting off the bus in the middle of what Nikki probably sees as a poverty stricken war-zone, I'll also have to drag nanna's shopping trolley behind me.

Nikki waves out of the window as the bus pulls away.

"She seemed like a nice girl." My nanna says. "Pity she has to use such coarse language." It's a good job nanna can't hear how the kids at school talk most of the time. It'd probably turn her hair black again. She also sounds amused, though, as if she knows how much I like Nikki! She's read my mind and now she knows! I hope she doesn't say anything to mam.

* *
* *

"We saw Christopher's girlfriend on the bus!" Nanna says this before I've even finished dragging the shopping bags into the kitchen.

"Girlfriend?" Mam's voice is dripping with sarcasm. "I doubt that. Look at him!" Mam sits in her chair while we put the shopping away. At some point she'll probably find something that we forgot to buy, or that we've bought the wrong type of something that she wanted. For now, however, she's got me and my 'girl-friend' to talk about. "And anyway, I've ruined him for any girl! He's too lazy. He'll never find anybody who'll run around after him like I do! You should see the state of his bedroom....."

I don't interrupt her or argue with her. I know there's not much point.

I wonder what Nikki thinks about our house and where we live. It could've been worse. One night, last Summer, our neighbours' dog barked at an old woman and she had a heart attack or something from fright. It was awful. The old woman's husband was kneeling next to her shouting;

"Call an ambulance, call a bloody ambulance" – but our neighbour just stood there laughing because he thought she'd fallen over drunk! Mam sat in the living room and went on and on about what a hell-hole we live in, and what a pig my dad is for making us live here in the first place. I didn't think our street was that bad until mam went on and on about it. She kept saying that we don't belong here, that we should've left years ago and that dad should've taken us to Australia like Auntie Pat's husband did. I went to bed early, but I could still hear people laughing in the street outside.

Last week, our next door neighbour knocked and asked if we wanted to buy any dog food. I told her that we don't have a dog, but she said it was Ok for cats to eat it too. I told her that we don't have a cat either so she left looking stroppy. Anyway, nanna reckoned it was in the local paper that four hundred pounds worth of food had been stolen from the local dog rescue shelter. I told my mam and I thought it was quite funny, but she flew off the handle again and said;

"It's bad enough that we have to live in a slum without you making jokes about it! Thieves living next door and you think it's funny!" Things are pretty black and white to my mam. I remember when my brother got beaten up by two of the bigger kids at school. They'd called him a '*queer*' and a '*homo*' and they'd taken his school bag off him and emptied it in the Burn. My mam had sat on the settee with her arms around him saying: "we should have had you away from here years ago, you're too good for this bloody place." She held him like he was still a baby. She'd called the Police and that just made things worse because they couldn't do very much about *'teenagers fighting'* and then I started getting picked on at school because everyone said I was a grass because I'd had to make a statement. And then the same kids started calling me a *'queer'* as well. The last time my brother was home we went down the town and we both got shouted at by some kids because Rob was wearing a straw hat and had his jumper tied round his waist. It was the usual words; 'puff', 'homo' and then they started singing; "who's the bender in the hat?" My brother said we just had to ignore them 'til they got bored and found somebody else to pick on. He hasn't been home since but I still have to go to the town.

I haven't told mam or nanna about cross country and the mud and the telling off I got at school yesterday. I don't see much point in talking about it. My nanna will just assume that I must've done something wrong, and my mam will tell me that I was probably hanging around with the wrong type of kids. It'd be even worse if they took my side. I can just imagine my nanna going up to school to tell Mr. Parr off. She used to work as a dinner nanny at a comprehensive and she can't half give people a dressing down when she wants to. Maybe Nixon will write to my mam. I don't honestly think that being covered in mud during a P.E. lesson is going to wreck my future, but some of those teachers would like to think so. Mam and nanna can do without the worry, anyway.

Does Nikki speak to her parents about me? How does she describe me? Does she ever think about me when I'm not with her?

I can't stop thinking about her.

Looking For Atlantis

Letter to that woman off the telly

46 Sampson Place
Newton Aycliffe
County Durham

Dear Norma,

I realise I'm not supposed to write to you directly, but I've tried writing to the address that they put up at the end of your programme but nobody ever replies. I'm also sure that you'll want to get personally involved in this case, as it will make your programme even more popular!

My mother and I watch 'Wildest Dreamz' every Sunday night – and we both really enjoy it. It seems to have something for everyone – there's a game show so people can win prizes, you have those awards for people who've had to overcome horrible tragedies – but the bit that we enjoy the most is always the last bit of your programme.

We love it when you reunite people with long lost relatives or friends. I'm a boy and I don't mind saying that I often have a good cry when old people meet up with family members that they thought were dead. I bet it's the most popular part of your show and I've got a story that you could use.

My mam is a twin – but she hasn't seen her sister for over twenty years (not since before I was born!). You see, her twin sister married an insurance salesman and they went to live in Australia. At first they kept in touch, but I think they must have moved house or something because they stopped answering our letters. My mam always talks about her sister and how she wishes she'd gone out to Australia instead of

67

settling down in England. I have cousins that I've never even met, and it would be great to find out about them.   My mam is quite ill so she can't work and we don't have much money coming in. We probably won't get the chance to visit my Auntie. I know it would make her feel a lot better if you could get them together on your show, or send us to Australia so that she could see her twin again! Just think how fantastic that would be! I bet the story would get into newspapers and magazines, too – somebody could probably write a book about it!

I really hope you can help – I'm looking forward to seeing everybody get back together again on your show.

Yours sincerely,

Christopher Mason

Looking For Atlantis

Friday, away from home

"You were supposed to have the proper boots," Mr. McPherson closes his eyes as he speaks to me. I think he's trying to show that he's exasperated.

"I always wear these to go walking in," I say, quite truthfully. I have a pair of trainer boots that I bought for a fiver in Shoe-Land in town. The only walking I do is to school or into town – but he's not to know that. For all he knows I could be up a mountain every weekend.

"They aren't gonna keep the rain out," he shrugs as if he's washing his hands of the whole matter. "If they fall to bits and you get pneumonia don't come crying to me, son." I hate it when teachers call me 'son.' I almost feel like saying; "Don't worry, I won't, *Dad*."

My boots are comfy enough. I really don't know how water-proof they are but I'm wearing three pairs of socks so it shouldn't be too much of a problem.

We got to the Youth Hostel just after seven this evening, and McPherson wanted to check our walking gear for tomorrow. He's got a big pile of school-bought waterproof coats and trousers, but he hasn't got any spare walking boots. Most people have brought the right stuff, but I'll be wearing one of the dark green school cagoules. McPherson has only brought one size – absolutely massive – so I'm probably going to spend most of the weekend looking like a tent.

Both my mam and my nanna kept talking about this weekend as if I was going on holiday to the other side of the world for six months. I kept telling them it's not a big deal but they did their best to make me feel awful.

"It's all right for some people," my mam said, "clearing off on holiday for the weekend."

"It's a school trip," I insisted, pointlessly, "we have to measure the depths of rivers and stuff like that."

"Listen to him! Complaining about his long weekend away!"

"We're only going for two nights!" I felt like I should've mentioned my brother and the fact that we haven't seen him at all for nearly eight months, but I know it's pointless saying bad things about him.

"Two nights away and he's not happy! I'd jump at the chance to get away to the Lake District for two nights!"

"I always thought I'd retire to somewhere like that," my nanna had chimed in, "no noise, no traffic – just a nice little cottage with one of them proper fires."

"You wouldn't last five minutes," I said, "you can't get a telly reception up there. No Corrie or Eastenders."

"Cheeky beggar," my nanna tutted, "we never had the bally television or half the things you've got when I was your age. We had to make our own amusement – we couldn't lock ourselves away with books and music. I had to share a room with five of my sisters! We had to spend most of our time out in the fresh air!"

"But that's what I'm doing this weekend! We're going to be halfway up a mountain!"

"And you're still complaining!"

The argument went round and round all week. I did feel a bit guilty because my nanna was staying in with my mam on Friday night instead of going to the Bingo. I had to keep telling myself that it's only one weekend, and it's not like I go away all the time. I also knew that my nanna would have to do the shopping on Saturday – and my mam would be disgusted because nanna always buys the cheapest supermarket own brand stuff. It's not like I buy expensive stuff – but my nanna goes out of her way to save a penny here and there. When she's at home, she actually does the shopping in three or four different shops just to compare the prices of baked beans. She says that it's all the same stuff – just in different packets, but she once bought some really cheap tins of Ravioli and it stank like dog food and sick.

I carried my bags up to school this afternoon. Just about everyone else was getting dropped off by parents.

"Why didn't you say something?" Nikki was a bit stroppy when she first saw me – I was puffing and panting and all red-faced after lugging my stuff up the bank. "My dad gave me a lift – we could've picked you up!"

"That's OK," I said, mentally kicking myself repeatedly in the head for not thinking of it. I could've met her dad! I could've been polite and sensible and made a good impression and then maybe her Dad would tell her that I was a 'nice young man' and Nikki would start to imagine me as possible boyfriend material! Then again, I'd have had my mam and nanna staring out of the kitchen window at her.

The mini-bus is a wreck. It's supposed to be white, but it's got long lines of rust on the doors and around the windows. It takes ages to drag the sliding door open. The seats are covered in graffiti that must be at least ten years old. I don't recognise any of the scrawled names. Before the journey, we had to bundle our belongings behind the seats and try to get comfortable.

"It smells of mould in here," David said as we tried to fold ourselves into the seats, and he was spot on. "There's not much room for me legs, either." David's taller than me, and he had to sit with his knees pushed up in front of him.

"How old is this thing?" Brian picked at a flake of rust above the door. A big chunk came away in his hand.

"Stop complaining!" McPherson was in a dreadful mood. He was frowning all the time we were in the mini-bus and he looked as if he was having to concentrate really hard on where we were going. Miss. Hobbs just went to sleep.

"It's pretty shocking though, isn't it, sir?" Brian never knew when to leave it alone. McPherson ignored him. "I bet if the Maths department wanted a mini-bus they'd get a better one than this..." McPherson still didn't bite so Brian started looking through his bag for his headphones.

Brian's never had any respect for any of the teachers, but he really goes to town on McPherson. He once told me that he has to liven up Geography because it's such a crappy lesson.

"Soft git always wears pink shirts," Brian said, "I mean, what sort of bloke wears pink shirts?" Just last week Brian tried to turn one of McPherson's lessons upside down.

McPherson had drawn this really detailed map of northern Europe on the board and he told us all to copy it into our text books. It's the usual boring stuff teachers get us to do at the start of lessons to try and calm us down. Anyway, McPherson disappeared into the cupboard at the back of his room – probably looking for atlases or something – and Brian went out to the board and rubbed 'France' off the map. Instead, he got one of the board pens and wrote '*Pink Shirt Land*'. The stupid thing was, nobody in the class laughed. Janice, "*her ladyship*", tutted, but nobody else reacted at all. McPherson came out of the cupboard with a pile of books and didn't even notice what Brian had done! Brian was obviously a bit gutted – so he kept asking McPherson questions like:

"Sir, do we have to copy the map down *exactly* as it is on the board?"

"Yes Brian." McPherson didn't look at the map. Brian got more and more agitated.

"But do we have to write down *every single one* of the labels?"

"Yes Brian – copy it into your book, just as it is on the board!" McPherson didn't have a clue what was going on – and none of us lot were laughing – so Brian had to go for broke.

"So sir, do we have to write PINK SHIRT LAND in our books?" Brian was grinning and looking around the room, waiting for us all to appreciate how brilliant and funny he was. Nobody even flickered. Apart from McPherson. He finally looked at his lovely map.

"Oh Brian," he said, sounding really disappointed, "don't do it. Don't do it in my lessons." He does this mad flickery eye-lid thing when he gets worked up, and he did it loads at Brian on that day. "Just get on with your work, son."

Brian also tries to wind McPherson up about having curly hair, the yellow comb that he always has in his back pocket, and anything else he can think of. It's the only time I've ever seen a pupil bully a teacher. Maybe Brian knows that McPherson can't do much about it.

The last time Brian tried to wind up one of the other kids he got his head kicked in. He'd been hassling somebody because their dad had been sent to prison. Brian got jumped on in the toilets and ending up peeing all over his own trousers.

Anyway, most people on the bus were listening to tiny mp3 players, or fiddling with mobile phones. Not many of us bothered talking to each other.

"I'm gonna miss the match tomorrow," David said. He goes to every single Darlington home game.

"I don't know why you bother," sneered Brian, "bunch of losers." I don't know much about football – but I do know that Darlington are in the bottom division. David persuaded me to go to one of the games with him a couple of weeks ago. I spent the whole game terrified that there was going to be a violent football riot. As it turned out, there weren't any hooligans – just a load of blokes eating pies in the rain.

"It's my local team," David retorted, "that's why I support them."

"They need all the bloody help they can get!" Brian chuckled.

"Exactly, it's up to the fans to keep the club going. They don't all get loads of TV money off Sky." David paused – he looked at me, and I knew straightaway what was coming next. "What team do you support, Bri, anyway?"

"Man United," Brian said, "always have, always will."

"That's amazing," David smiled.

"What is?"

"I never knew you came from Manchester. You haven't got a Manc accent – so when did your family move up here?" David is one of the few people who can wind Brian up. It's because he sounds so reasonable all the time, so Brian doesn't feel as if he's having the mickey taken out of him.

"I'm not from Manchester. Bloody awful place."

"Oh – right. I just thought, you know – if you support Man U…"

"I've always liked Man U," Brian snapped, "I've always watched their games."

"On the telly?"

"Aye – well Old Trafford's very expensive."

"Still, it must be nice to support a team that wins so many trophies…" This went on for a while, until Brian shut up and finally put his headphones on. David turned to me and mouthed: "Glory hunter."

I looked around the bus – Nikki was sitting a couple of rows back, her eyes closed and her headphones on.

"You shouldn't wind Brian up," I said to David.

"Why the hell not?"

"He's cooking your breakfast."

Looking For Atlantis

Saturday Morning

It turns out that Brian is a wizard in the kitchen. He stands cracking eggs and frying bacon, stirring beans and turning sausages. He's even wearing one of those novelty aprons with a semi-naked woman on the front.

"I must say, I'm impressed," Miss. Hobbs looks over at Brian. His hands are a blur as he concentrates on sorting breakfast out.

"Ready for a plate, over here!" Brian yells at me and David to bring stuff to him. He clicks his fingers when he needs something. If he wasn't cooking so much gorgeous looking stuff, I'd probably tell him to stick it.

I didn't think I'd like a fried breakfast but it smells brilliant. I have a theory about stuff like this – it's like when you walk past a fish and chip shop – it smells fantastic and it makes your mouth water, but the food never lives up to the smell. I mean, what do fish and chips actually taste of apart from salt and vinegar? Everybody remembers the smell and wanting to eat them more than the actual taste. And I always feel sick afterwards because I've eaten them so fast. Anyway, not even David is complaining about the way Brian is talking to us. We're both stood there, practically drooling as Brian works his magic.

"Who'd have thought that Brian is actually good for something?" David says.

"His girl-friend must see something in him." It's always bothered me that most of the kids I know who are badly behaved or really annoying always seem to have girl-friends and I never do.

"Love is blind," David mutters, "and Brian's girl-friend must have lost her white stick."

David is my best friend at school and has been for quite a while. I'm not sure if I'm *his* best friend, but he's certainly mine. We got talking because I asked him if he wanted some cartoons drawing for the school magazine. David is the editor – but it's not an '*official*' school magazine, and the teachers aren't supposed to see it because he writes articles about how pointless the school rules are, and which teachers have been seen in the local pub at lunch-time. He also thinks that more intelligent pupils should be allowed to 'opt out' of lessons like PE, PSHE, and RE because they are a complete waste of time. He pays to have the magazine photocopied at the stationery shop in Darlington. I don't know how much it costs him, but he doesn't seem to care. He hands copies out for free at school and says that he has to "spread the word." He writes very clever stuff. He knows all about human rights and what's going on in the news all over the world. He reads newspapers and watches Channel 4 a lot. It was after reading his magazine that I started writing letters. I've even used some of his ideas and tried to sound grown up like he does when he talks about things.

When we first became friends I taped him the first two Prefab Sprout albums. He seemed quite keen after I told him that not many people had heard of them but he gave me the tape back and said they were "too commercial" and he gave me a tape with some Manic Street Preachers songs on it. I couldn't get into them at all.

Anyway, I started doing some cartoons for David's magazine. He seemed to like them. I invented a character called '*The Bad Dog.*' The Bad Dog comic strips always follow the same pattern. They are only three panels long, and in the first picture, somebody is happy; they've just won the lottery or gotten married or something. In the second picture, The Bad Dog appears, and says something like;

"Yeah, you may have won the lottery, but now people will only be your friend because they want you to buy them things."

The third and last picture shows the lottery winner surrounded by money, but with their head in their hands, saying;

"Now life is worse than ever!"

Every strip is pretty much the same. Somebody thinks they're going to be happy but The Bad Dog turns up and says something to ruin it. David thinks that my comic strips say something "important about values in modern Britain," but I just like drawing the dog. He's not a difficult character to draw, to be honest – it's just four match-stick legs with a big head. He looks more like a cat with the head of a Teddy Bear, which might explain why he's a 'Bad Dog' in more ways than one.

"I wonder what he's going to make for our tea?" David asks as we wipe our greasy plates with bread and butter.

"I don't know... but we did offer to do the washing up." I look at the pans and plates that are swimming in lard and shudder, and I know just how long it's going to take to scrape the fat off.

The Youth Hostel kitchen is huge, and there are loads of people milling about, making toast, drinking tea or reading newspapers at the big wooden tables. Most of us lot from the school trip look really tired because we didn't arrive 'til late and then we sat up half the night talking.

Another letter To Auntie Pat

46 Sampson Place
Newton Aycliffe
County Durham

Dear Auntie Pat,

How are you? The post seems to take ages from Australia! We haven't had any from you in months. I hope your letters haven't got lost over the sea!

I hope you are all happy and healthy. Things didn't go too well at the hospital for mam the other day. The specialist says they can give her a boost with some medicine and help her with some pain-killers but there's no longer term plan.

I've been reading up about mam's illness at the library and it says that being in a warmer climate might help. Is it really sunny every single day in Australia? It might be the perfect place for mam to live – what do you think?

I've been thinking about it, and I think it would also do her good to see you again – she's always saying how much she misses you. Nanna says that you have a big house so maybe mam could come and stay with you until we could afford our own place out there. I'm still doing well at school so I should be able to get a good job. Maybe I could come and work for Uncle Pete. That would be great! Let me know what you think!

I must go – I'm away for the weekend on a Geography trip and the mini-bus is leaving any second. I want to post this letter before they take us walking in the hills! I've wrapped up warm because we're in the Lake District – and it's nothing like Australia!

Lots of love
Chris.

Looking For Atlantis

Saturday afternoon

"Are they clouds?" Parky is looking down into a valley. There's a thick mist rolling between the mountains and you can just see odd bits of rock and grass sticking through.

"How high up do you think we are?" David asks him.

"I don't know. I've just never seen anything like it." We've stopped at the top of some mountain, High-Scarthen-something or other, and we've been told we can have our packed lunches here. There are a couple of benches and stones to sit on – but everything is pretty damp. It doesn't matter all that much because we're all completely soaked. It was just starting to drizzle when we left the Youth Hostel this morning, and we've enjoyed pretty much non-stop rain ever since we started walking. We had to take it in turns to carry the haversack, so I went first because I knew I'd be too knackered later on. The waterproof coats they've given us are making me sweat loads. I can feel the plasticky material clammy against my neck and arms. I hope my roll-on deodorant works otherwise I'm going to be stinking by the end of the day. Mr. McPherson keeps telling us to look at 'drumlin swarms' and 'nunataks' as if they're supposed to be important.

"My brother is a total nutter," Nikki tells me, "he's at University in Glasgow and every weekend he sends me picture messages of him and his mates. He joined one of them Social Societies they have at Universities – they pretend they're interested in sports or politics or books, but really they just go out and get drunk!"

"Oh, right."

"Aye – they all complain about not having much money – but they always seem to have plenty for drink!" Nikki laughs. "He's always having to ask for extra time to do his essays and he misses loads of lectures because he's got a hangover! It sounds like he's having a brilliant time!"

"Yeah, I bet he is." University doesn't sound like much fun to me. It sounds like it's all about drinking. My mam has told me about some of the things that dad used to do after he'd been out drinking with his Police mates. Once, he thought their wardrobe was a toilet - and another time he fell through the glass door in the living room. He had to have thirty stitches in his arm. I wonder if he remembers those things as being part of a 'good night out.'

"Where's your brother at?" Nikki asks. Somebody must've told her that he's at University because I've never mentioned him.

"He went to Durham."

"Really? That's not far away!" She laughs. "When I go to University I'm going to go as far away from home as I can! I bet your brother comes home every weekend with his dirty washing, does he?"

"Actually he only comes home at Christmas," I tell her, "he says he's got so many essays to write and I think he does some theatre group or something..."

"It's only twenty minutes on the bus..." Nikki says.

"I know, but my mam tells him to save his money – she says he needs to make sure he sticks in and gets a good job at the end of it."

"Well she's right, I suppose."

"Yeah." I want to tell her that my brother couldn't wait to get away from home and he's left me to deal with everything and I hate him for staying away but I don't want her to think I'm angry or bitter or jealous.

I've spent most of the day falling over. My boots don't have enough grips on them to keep me upright. I've been stuck at the back of our group – but that's turned out to be a brilliant thing. Nikki has been hanging back with me – and she keeps falling over too!

"It must be love!" David had laughed because he'd seen me and Nikki fall over at exactly the same time!

"I don't suppose anybody expected fatty Mason to keep up," Nobby had said as Nikki and I caught up with the rest of the group at the top of the mountain. Some of the other kids laughed. I don't care.

"I can't believe how childish this lot are," Nikki said to me as we walked this morning. "They were so excited about getting away for the weekend – all going on about trying to smuggle boys back into the dorm or going out to buy alcohol. It's like being out with a load of ten year olds!" I agreed with everything Nikki said. To be honest though, I was so exhausted after the first ten minutes of walking that I could barely talk anyway. I just sort of grunted and nodded a lot.

It is pretty amazing out here. It's raining and it's misty and it feels like we're miles from anywhere. I can't get used to the quiet. Apart from our own voices and the slippy sliding noises we make on the wet ground there isn't any other noise to speak of. No cars. I haven't heard any planes going by. It's probably too late in the year for there to be any birds. It's almost like we've landed on a different planet. I haven't thought about school or mam or nanna. I just want to talk to Nikki. She smiles and she laughs a lot. Is it love? I don't know what it's supposed to feel like. How can you tell? Maybe these funny feelings are just me being happy. How do people know when they're happy or when they're not? Most people make their minds up afterwards and only realise that they used to be happy once something has made them miserable.

****
****

"'Ow, sir!" Brian has shuffled forward so that he's in the seat directly behind McPherson. "Stick the radio on, it's five to five and the footy results should be coming through!"

We've been back in the bus for about five minutes and everyone is pretty knackered. There are a lot of red faces and wet feet.

"Brian," McPherson says patiently, "it's really not a good idea to distract me while I'm driving..." Some of the roads are really narrow and wind round and round the mountainsides. McPherson's knuckles are white as he grips the steering wheel.

"Oh go on, sir, I want to find out how United got on at Blackburn..." Realising that he won't get any peace, McPherson jabs the car stereo and we can hear one of those boring voiced blokes reading out the scores. Brian sits in silence – until he finds out that United won one nil. "Come on you reds! Come on you reds!" Brian starts pointing his finger in the air and then clapping his hands.

"Brian!" McPherson barks. "I am driving!"

"But sir – we're six points clear!"

"It's only November, "David reminds him.

"And how did Darlo do today?"

"If you shut up, I might be able to hear..." They lost. Four nil at home.

"Ah well, it's only November," says Brian, with a daft grin.

"That's the point of following a team," says David, "you support them when they're playing crap – not just when they're winning trophies..."

"When did Darlo ever win a trophy? It sounds like bollocks to me..."

"Brian!" McPherson yells and the mini-bus swerves. "Remember where you are, son!"

I'm sitting behind Brian and David – and Nikki is asleep next to me. I think all that walking has really taken it out of her. I've thought about putting my arm around her so she doesn't fall off the seat, but if she woke up suddenly she might think I'm a perv. I'd probably be asleep too, but the rain-water has finally managed to get through my three pairs of socks and my toes feel like icicles. Before she fell asleep,

Nikki said that I could use her mobile phone to call my mam if I wanted. She knows I'm worried about leaving her over the weekend. I haven't told her what's wrong – I've just said she's not very well at the moment. I didn't tell Nikki that we don't have the phone on at home – I just said my nanna was taking care of everything so I didn't really need to call.

"Sir, what team do you support?" David asks this question and then nods at Brian.

"Chelsea – best team in the world."

"Really?" David sounds surprised. "I didn't realise you came from London."

"I don't – I grew up near Sheffield, but I've *always* supported Chelsea." Brian butts in:

"So why don't you support Sheffield United or Wednesday?" He's obviously found a new way to wind McPherson up. David grins. The mini-bus trundles on.

Saturday Evening

"You'd think they'd at least have a bloody telly."
David is not happy. There's not a lot to do at the Youth
Hostel. Some of the lads are playing pool and darts in the
games room – and most of the girls must be hiding up in their
dormitory. Me and David are sitting in these really
uncomfortable wooden-armed chairs in the lounge. "There's
footy on tonight."

"It wouldn't matter anyway. You can't get a reception
up here because of all the mountains." The lounge is like the
inside of a brown shoe. It can't have been decorated in
decades.

"They could have had cable or satellite put in – like
they do in pubs."

"Might be nice to not have telly," I suggest, "no
crappy talent shows, no soaps, no Big Brother – you'd
probably have to read more books, speak to people, go for
walks and stuff."

"I don't know if I could hack it," David says dryly,
"no footy!" David is pretty funny. It was only a couple of
weeks ago that he turned up for school with no hair. He
shaved it all off because people kept taking the mickey out of
him for being ginger. It's still really short – he's just got dark
patches of stubble all over his head.

He also buys most of his clothes from Army Surplus
shops. He doesn't want to be in the army, he just likes having
lots of pockets. Mrs. Nixon dragged him out of assembly and
yelled at him for wearing combat trousers to school. He told
her that they were black trousers and therefore perfectly in
keeping with the school uniform policy. She was having none
of it. She sent him home and rang his dad.

David doesn't take much crap from teachers. The
Deputy Head yelled at him for wearing a hammer and sickle
Soviet badge in the corridor. Mr. Block (which is funny

because he does actually have a square head) asked him if he was aware of 'the political significance of the emblem'. David reckons he gave Block a five minute mini-lecture on the Russian Revolution and the Communist Manifesto. David also asked Block if he really had time to hassle people about badges, especially when there were so many pupils to teach and bullies to discipline. Block excluded him for five days.

David's parents don't seem to get worked up about him getting letters home and stuff like that. It's almost as if they approve of him standing up for himself and challenging authority. I couldn't talk to teachers like David does. He always seems to have a smart answer. I just try to keep my head down.

"It's bang out of order," David spits, and I suddenly realise that I haven't been listening to him.

"What is?"

"McPherson and Hobbs have cleared off to a pub to watch the footy – leaving us to enjoy precisely bugger-all!"

"Well, it's not as if they could take us. None of us are old enough."

"That's not the point! They can't just leave us without any supervision – we could be having orgies or something. It stinks." I just nod my head. I'm now expecting a full-blown rant about how elitist and awful our teachers are.

"You two look happy!" Nikki beams as she sits down next to me. She's appeared from nowhere.

"Oh, erm, David was just telling me about our corrupt rulers…"

"Eh?" Nikki frowns. "I always seem to miss the fun conversations!" I've always wanted to meet a sarcastic girl! David stands up.

"Well, I'm going to go and ring home – I might have to tell my mam about our runaway teachers," he smiles at me, "and I have no intention of playing gooseberry!" He makes loud kissing noises as he leaves.

"What's he on about?" I've never seen David do stuff like that before.

"Just ignore him," Nikki sighs, brushing a stray hair from her face. "Have you recovered from the mountains yet?"

"Yeah, well, you know, just about." I try to chuckle and smile, but I probably just sound as if I'm choking.

"At least we had good weather, eh?" She's really smiling and her eyes are shiny. I just sit there with a big daft grin on my face. I must be blushing like crazy. I can't believe that Nikki came over to speak to me.

Brian and some of his mates wander through the lounge. He wolf-whistles loudly as he passes us, and Parky starts singing '*Love is in the Air.*'

"Oh for Christ's sake," Nikki groans, "let's go for a walk."

****

The Lake is pitch black. We can hear the rustling of the water as it laps up against the shore, but we can't really see anything. There aren't any boats or lights out there and the weather is remarkably still, considering how crappy it was earlier on.

But it's still cold.

"It's lovely," Nikki says, "so peaceful and quiet." I just wish we'd grabbed our coats before we came out. "And look at the stars!" I look up and the sky is dotted with tiny pin-heads of light.

"I think that one's a planet!" I point at a flickery red light. "It might be Mars – you're supposed to be able to see other planets on a clear night."

"D'you think that comet will be gone by now?" I almost faint. Nikki is the only other person I know who has shown any interest in the comet. It's amazing how much in common we have. It's starting to feel like fate has brought us together. "I saw it last week-end."

"I dunno, it might've moved on by now."

"Oh well, I'll have to try and catch it again next time." We stand there in silence for a bit, smiling at our own private little joke. It's brilliant! How cool are we?

I want to tell her that I sometimes leave my bedroom curtains open on clear nights. I have my bed right under the window so I can look up at the stars. I like to think of them as being in 3-D. It's not as if they're all painted on a big window – they're all at different distances away from us – looking at it I like to imagine that I can travel through them. I want to tell her this and maybe then she'll say that she does the same thing and then we'll realise that we are meant for each other!

"Some of those stars are dead," Nikki frowns, "some of them died before we were born!"

"Some of those stars were dead before our grand-parents were born. It takes ages for that light to reach us." Is this what people talk about? Is this small talk? Shouldn't we just talk about the weather – rather than life, death and the Universe? It does feel like we're standing right on the edge – not just of the galaxy and the stars, but on the edge of everything, as the lights from the past catch up with us through little holes in the sky. I wish there was some way I could say what I'm thinking to Nikki – without sounding dead soft.

"If I had my coat on," I say, noticing that Nikki is shivering, "I'd offer it to you."

"So! Chivalry isn't dead!"

"I do try. I just haven't got my coat on at the minute. I am thinking chivalrous thoughts."

"I'm glad to hear it!"

So would this be a good moment to tell her that I like her? With this big starry back-drop and my excellent manners – should I, could I, tell her that I think I'm falling in love with her? Of course, I can't be certain that I am in love – I don't know what it's supposed to feel like because I've never done it before. I'm not sleeping very well, I'm not eating as much as I used to and I get butterflies in my stomach every time I'm

near her. Those sorts of things should make me feel terrible –
but it's a nice kind of terrible I'm feeling right now.

"Prefab Sprout," is what I eventually say.

"Eh?"

"Prefab Sprout – they're my favourite band. They
made a whole album of songs about stars." I wish I'd brought
that tape with me. "Every song they've ever done is perfect
but there's one on that album about how being weightless and
floating about in space is exactly like being in love." I hope
it's true. I hope feelings like this go on and on and into outer
space forever.

"You'll have to do me a copy." I wish I could tell
whether or not she's being sarcastic.

"And there's another one about a bloke who's
prepared to visit every star in the sky just to find his one true
love. He knows that she's got to be out there somewhere." I
think for a minute and listen to the water sloshing about
against the shore. "I mean, it's romantic rubbish I suppose,
but I like it – it's old-fashioned."

"Well, it's no wonder then, is it?"

"What – do you think I'm old-fashioned?"

"You've just said you'd give me your coat – if you'd
been wearing one. Good manners," she grins, "are *incredibly*
old-fashioned nowadays."

I can't work out if she means this is good thing or not.
Anyway, the night isn't getting any warmer, and we've
started to drift back towards the lights of the Youth Hostel. I
think I'm definitely in love. I should tell her. If it's really love
and I really do mean it, then there can't be any harm in telling
her, can there? And I want to tell her everything. I want to tell
her about my mam and my dad and Auntie Pat in Australia
and my letters to the mayor... And I want to sit her down and
play her Prefab Sprout records because Paddy McAloon puts
these feelings into words better than I can.

Letter to the Bank

46 Sampson Place
Newton Aycliffe
County Durham

Dear Sir,

Thank you for taking the time to read this correspondence. I realise that you must get lots of requests for help in your line of work, but I hope you will give my proposal serious consideration.

I am an account holder at your branch in Newton Aycliffe town centre, and I currently deposit at least one pound per month in my account – it tends to be more if I get money for my birthday or at Christmas. If you look into your records you will see that I am regular customer and my account has always been in credit.

The reason I am writing is to ask you if it would be possible to take out a loan. My mother has a serious illness and it is her wish to visit her twin sister in Australia. Unfortunately, she is unable to work due to her illness and I am unable to seek employment due to the fact that I am still at school. I am proposing that I loan the money from your bank to cover the costs of my mam's trip to Australia, and I will be able to pay it back once I am old enough to have a job. I am an able pupil at school (I can submit written reports from my teachers if you wish) and I expect to find employment in a well paid profession. Paying the loan back will not be a problem and the bank can make money by charging me interest in the mean time.

I realise that my request is unusual, but if I wait until I am old enough to find a job, my mother may not be well enough to travel.

I do hope that you will give my idea some thought and respond as soon as is convenient. I am a reliable and loyal customer to your bank.

Yours faithfully

Christopher Mason

Looking For Atlantis

Sunday Morning

It's just after 2am when McPherson bursts into the dormitory.

"I have had enough!" He hisses through clenched teeth. I'm sure he'd be yelling his head off if the rest of the Youth Hostel wasn't fast asleep by now. "I am sick and tired of the stupid noises coming from you lot!"

Brian has been making farty noises by blowing raspberries onto the back of his hand. They have been very, very loud.

"Those noises aren't even realistic! And if you do need the toilet – *just go* – you don't need to *advertise* the fact!" We've all been hiding under our bed covers since McPherson stomped in, but I know for a fact that everybody in the room is helpless with laughter.

Parky and Ollie had orange squash mixed with vodka this evening, so they'll laugh at anything – added to that, McPherson has switched the light on, so we all got a glimpse of him in his stripy t-shirt and grey skimpy briefs. I'm actually gnawing on my own knuckles to stop myself from cracking up.

The five of us in our little dorm haven't had any sleep. We started talking about school, then the teachers (do we think McPherson and Hobbs are sharing a room?), and before we knew it Brian was doing his usual clown routine. We managed to persuade him to stop shouting '*fire*' but then he started on with the farty noises.

"If any of you can't be quiet," McPherson rages, "then you'll have to come into my room and sleep with me!" He switches the light off and leaves – and he must be able to hear us all laughing. David's laughing so hard he smacks his head off the bed frame and I'd be surprised if Brian hasn't wet himself.

Brian had sidled up to me while he'd been warming up our 'pies-in-tins' earlier on.

"Still getting on well with the new girl?" Brian has had a girl-friend since he was about eleven. She's in the year below ours, but since they've been going out for a few years, nobody bothers winding him up about being a *'cradle snatcher'* anymore. I still don't quite know how people get girl-friends, never mind keep them for so long.

"Ey! She's all right, she is," said Ollie. "I quite fancy her!" I must've been blushing or something because Brian and Ollie both started laughing and saying more stuff about how I must be in love with Nikki. I was just pleased she wasn't around to hear it all.

"Are you going with her, then?" Brian asked.

"Don't be daft," I said, "she wouldn't look at me."

"I dunno, she seems to like you and she talks to you all the time."

"She doesn't really know anyone," I told him, which is exactly what I'd been telling myself, "I'm one of the few people she's met so of course she speaks to me a lot. Once she's been here a bit longer, she'll probably…"

"I'd get in there if I was you." I don't know what Brian means. How do I get 'in there'? What am I supposed to do? We have had some good chats and we've walked home from school together a couple of times – but what do I do to move things on? "Because somebody else will." That was a great thing for him to say.

Anyway, we sat with David and ate our pies-in-tins with some bread and butter. I'd been put in charge of buttering the bread and then doing the washing up. Brian used the tin opener and lifted stuff in and out of the oven. He must've been too tired to repeat his breakfast time heroics. David said he'd do us some toast and tea in the morning.

Will somebody else ask Nikki out? What if she gets
sick of waiting for me? What if she thinks I'm not interested?
Oh God.

Love Is In The Air

They are late coming out of school. Mr McPherson has been running a revision class so it's nearly 4 o'clock by the time they emerge from the side entrance of the school. All of the other kids have already gone home. Winter is already in the air – the damp Autumn evening has a crisp bite to it.

Chris and Nikki walk across the school field and down towards the Burn together - they both have their big, bad-weather coats on, and they carry school-bags stuffed with Geography text-books and notes. They chuckle and chatter as they step carefully through the mist and mud. They discuss the day at school, Nikki giggling as Chris makes pointed and well observed comments about their class-mates and teachers.

Chris offers Nikki his arm so that she doesn't slip as they make their way down the slope towards the Burn bridge. She smiles, a beaming, radiant smile and her pale blue eyes light up at Chris' gentlemanly gesture. It wouldn't matter if they had left school on time and been surrounded by other pupils – Chris and Nikki are in a world of their own...

Suddenly, Nikki loses her footing on the bridge – she is about fall onto the wet wooden slats – but Chris is aware of the danger. He selflessly casts his school bag aside and gracefully catches Nikki in his arms.
"I've got you," he says, with a smile.
"Too right have you have," she replies. "I've been waiting for this for a long time..." She closes her eyes as he leans forward to kiss her.

Jesus. I can't get her out of my head.

I'll have to make sure I shred this in case my mam goes through my diary while I'm at school.

Looking For Atlantis

Sunday Afternoon

"What a waster!!!" David is not impressed with William Wordsworth. We're standing in the upstairs bedroom in Dove Cottage. There's a lot of dark wood in the house and old-fashioned fire-places and stuff. The ceilings are really low. Everybody must have been midgets four hundred years ago. Miss. Hobbs has been telling us all about the place and how Wordsworth had been left some money by a rich friend so he didn't have to work.

"It's like he was one of them scroungers on benefits, or one of them daft rich kids whose Daddy writes him cheques," David says, "he just sat around thinking and writing his daft poems instead of getting out and doing something useful."

"This part of the world inspired some of the greatest poetry ever written in the English language," Miss. Hobbs never gets angry. She looks at me: "you should ask your brother – I don't think I ever had a more insightful pupil write about poetry. He understood the importance of Wordsworth. His words should be treasured." I wonder if Paddy McAloon will have his lyrics studied by kids in the future. I reckon I could easily write an essay on the 'Steve McQueen' album.

"Aye, but I bet there were people starving nearby while he was poncing up and down the hills looking at flowers and that." Miss. Hobbs sighs and starts talking to some of the other kids. David is left fuming and kicking his heels.

"It must have been nice, though. I mean, they didn't have phones or electricity or anything – but they didn't know about things like that so they never would have wanted them." I don't think David is listening to me. "And living in the Lake District would've been mint! All that fresh air and scenery. They wouldn't even have had tourists or school parties!"

According to the handout Miss. Hobbs gives us, Wordsworth used to leave his curtains open so that he could look at the moon reflecting on the water. David sneers at this as "just the sort of thing a poet would do", but I can understand it. The stars must have been so much brighter back when Wordsworth saw them – they didn't have street lights or a bloody big industrial estate to spoil the view.

We sit on a wall beside Dove Cottage and eat sandwiches. Miss. Hobbs is in her element.

"Just look at the view!" It is pretty spectacular. Imagine waking up to this every morning. Imagine waking up to mountains, fields and cattle, instead of black fences, yellow bricked houses and pit-bulls. "Can't you see how this place inspired the poetry we've been reading?"

"I didn't get inspired very much yesterday," Brian says, "I just got wet feet and a ripped cagoule."

"He's such a philistine," Nikki mutters. I think I know what she means.

"Yes," I agree with her, "he's ignorant." I wonder if I should agree with her *all* the time. I wonder if that's what she'd like. Maybe she'd rather have sparks flying and arguments and stuff like that. I don't know. I wish we could just sit and hold hands and I could say something romantic.

"It's like that book we did in school, you know the one – '*Jane Eyre*'."

"Oh yeah?"

"I love anything by the Bronte sisters. They lived out in the wilds, too. Wuthering Heights and all that stuff."

"Right, yeah." I'm not saying much. She might start to think that I'm a philistine, too.

"I mean, it's old-fashioned and it's romantic and you could even say it's soppy, but it's just so nice to get lost in their books now and again."

"I suppose so," I say, still trying to decide if I should agree with everything she says. "I mean, it's OK to read, but it's not very realistic."

"But that's the point, isn't it? I don't want to read something that's realistic, something that could happen to me. Normal life is dead boring, so why read books about it? That'd be boring too!"

"Aye," she's got a point, but I'm not sure I agree. "Don't you think people get the wrong idea if all they read is stuff with happy endings? Life's not like that."

"I don't know if Jane Eyre has a happy ending…" I kick myself for not reading it again. I should've dug out my brother's essay so I could find out what it was all about and why it's so good. "I think most people realise the difference between real life and stories, Chris."

****

We're nearly home. There's a weird atmosphere in the Mini-bus because everybody's realised that we're heading back and that tomorrow we'll be back at school just like normal. It's a Boxing Day sort of feeling, I suppose. Brian has been listening to something loud and dreadful on his mp3 player, Janice (*'her ladyship'*) has been trying to do the cross-word in a Sunday Paper she bought this morning, Parky and Ollie have been sitting quietly at the back with green, hung-over faces, David has been trying to start a conversation about Third World Debt, Mr. McPherson and Miss. Hobbs have been discussing the "beautiful landscape", Nikki has been asleep, and I've just been sat here – not wanting the week-end to end.

David has also noticed that Mr. McPherson has been playing some music on the stereo. The mini-bus is too old to have a CD player, so he's got a stash of cassettes in the glove compartment.

"What sort of stuff do you like, sir?"

"All kinds," McPherson says, "this is a compilation, but I've got some Level 42, Texas, Simple Minds, proper music." I recognise one or two of those names from my dad's record collection.

"I love Texas," says Miss. Hobbs and David pulls a face.

"All those bands are a bit eighties though, aren't they?" says David. "You not got anything by Coldplay or The Killers?"

"I don't mind Coldplay," says McPherson, "they'd done a couple of good tunes." David cringes. Nothing makes a band un-cool like finding out your teacher likes them.

Another song starts on McPherson's tape, and I almost pass out with excitement. It's '*The King Of Rock'n'Roll*' by Prefab Sprout!

"That's a classic!" I blurt out. "Prefab Sprout!"

"You can't have heard of Prefab Sprout," McPherson says, "they're well before your time."

"Is that what they were called?" Miss. Hobbs says, "I'd forgotten all about this song. They were one of those one-hit wonder bands, weren't they?" I feel myself flushing scarlet.

"This was their biggest hit," I say, "but they had a few top 40 singles," I'm about to list '*When Love Breaks Down*', '*The Sound of Crying*' and '*If You Don't Love Me*,' but McPherson cuts me off;

"Aye – they were great! More of an albums band though – I used to have all of their stuff." I don't know whether to laugh or cry. "I saw them at Newcastle City Hall back when I was a student. Brilliant songs." David nudges me in the ribs and grins. Bloody hell. Bloody bloody hell. "Paddy McAloon is a genius."

I stay quiet for a long time.

****
****

"I've just got to make a phone call!" Mr. McPherson pulls the mini-bus over at a service station and hops out of the driver's side door. He mustn't have a mobile either. Just about everybody else (including Miss. Hobbs) has been texting or calling home to let parents and friends know what time we're due back.

"Who do you reckon he's calling?" Brian says – loudly.

"Wife? Girlfriend?"

"Boyfriend, more like," Bri laughs. "Nah – I bet he's just making one of them dirty phone calls."

"Brian," Janice (*'her ladyship'*) says, "you are such a child."

"I bet he is – he's dashed over because he's desperate to do a bit of heavy-breathing. What a perv!"

"I don't really think it's appropriate to discuss a member of staff in this manner," Miss. Hobbs says calmly, "I'm sure you wouldn't like to repeat your comments to Mr. McPherson when he returns."

"I'm not bothered," says Brian, and I know he's not. He'd probably take great delight in asking McPherson if he's a perv.

Sunday Evening

"I bet you've brought a load of dirty washing home with you!" I could tell as soon as I got home that things hadn't gone well. Mam was already in bed with a 'migraine' and my nanna was sitting on her own in the living room. She only ever puts one of the lamps on when she's sitting on her own. She was sipping tea and frowning.

"I'll sort it out," I told her. "There's not that much, I'll put it in the washer." The TV wasn't on. My nanna was just sitting there. "How have things been?" I asked.

"Quiet," she said, "ssssslurp-gulp-aaaaaah! Your mam hasn't been well so I've been on my own most of the weekend."

"What's been up with her?"

"Headaches, she says, I haven't put the telly on in case I disturb her." That's just silly. Mam's room isn't above the living room, so she wouldn't have heard the telly anyway. My nanna does stuff like this though. She hasn't put the telly on so that she can make herself even more miserable and make me feel bad for not being here.

"Has she heard from Rob?" It's my brother's birthday in a fortnight and we still don't know if he's coming home. He could at least tell us what he's going to do.

"Not a word." Maybe I should write to him, maybe I should tell him what I think of him. I should let him know how thoughtless and uncaring he looks. He's older than me – he could use his student loan or get an overdraft and pay for mam to go to Australia – I should tell him that he owes it to her to do that. But then he'd tell mam and I'd get told off for causing trouble. I'd just get the same old lecture about Rob having his whole future ahead of him.

I wonder if this is what jet-lag feels like. I feel weird. It's like the weekend didn't really happen and all my chats with Nikki were a dream. I've been away but then being back home makes me wish I'd never gone – simply because I had to come back. And then it's more school tomorrow.

Letter to the chef bloke off the telly

46 Sampson Place
Newton Aycliffe
County Durham

Dear Barry,

May I just take this opportunity to congratulate you on your recent win at the TV Awards. Many of my schoolfriends watch your programme and they all talk about it the day after it's been on. I always thought programmes about food and cooking would be boring for teenagers, but your no-nonsense attitude keeps them interested!

Anyway, the real reason I'm writing to you is because I've had an idea for a brilliant new show – and you would make the perfect host. I got the idea after watching you prepare that special meal for the Queen's birthday. I thought it was amazing how you and your team managed to cook for hundreds of people in one go. The Queen seems to have lots and lots of friends and you took care of every single one. I thought they were being really greedy, but as it turned out, some of the plates didn't actually have that much food on them.

So – my idea: I think it would be really good if you (and some of your other chef friends) went to some of those places in Eastern Europe or Africa where people don't get as much to eat as we do. If you can cook five or six courses for a couple of hundred people in Britain, just think how many meals you could cook for hungry people! And they wouldn't expect fancy table-cloths or cutlery, either! I'm sure they'd appreciate it. I know they couldn't expect some of them fancy starters that you do, or those expensive wines, but they'd love to have just a one course meal!

Looking For Atlantis

Maybe you could do a whole series where you could go and cook for a different village in Africa every week. I'm sure lots of people would watch it, and you might even get another TV award or even an OBE to go with the CBE you got for cooking the Queen's dinner!

I think a lot of your friends would like to help to. We had a situation like this in Food Technology last week. We had to make short-bread, which was quite straight-forward, but we are just learning. As we were finishing the lesson, Kevin Smith dropped his tray (it was dead hot after coming out of the oven) so all of his short-bread ended up on the floor. He was a bit upset because he'd done quite well up to that point. Mrs Rowe said that everybody else in the class should give Kevin one piece of short-bread each to make up for his accident. I know it sounds a bit obvious, but we all did it and I was really surprised because nobody complained. After giving Kevin once piece of my short-bread I still had fifteen pieces left to take home. Wouldn't it be great if everybody could do stuff like that more often?

Anyway, I'm sure you're busy with your restaurants and your TV shows, so I'll leave it there. Let me know what you think of my idea!

Yours sincerely
Christopher Mason

Monday

"But I just don't get it!" I say this as loudly as I can, just to be sure that Nikki is listening. I want to tell her about my letters and the stuff that I talk about with David, but it's Lunch-time in the school dining hall. It's bloody noisy. There are trays and knives and forks clattering about all over the place – and hundreds of conversations are happening all at the same time. Most of our year group have been talking about the week-end – and the story about Mr. McPherson shouting at us in his skimpy pants has quickly spread round the school.

"I said – I don't get it!"

"Eh?" She doesn't look up so I push my finger in front of her face and tap on the magazine article that she's reading.

"Him – that singer" I don't know his name "I think he plays the piano"

"You mean Johnny Marsden?" Nikki finally looks at me.

"Do I?"

"He's one of the most famous people on the planet!" she snorts "You must know Johnny Mardsen – he wrote 'Love Life Forever' – all of that slushy stuff that my mam likes".

"I know he's dead rich." I know who Johnny Marsden is - my dad left one of his singles behind. It was crap.

"He's been around for years – loads of people buy his records," then she adds, hurriedly, "not me, like – it's a bit cheesy, his stuff". Nikki might be a goth. She likes a lot of those loud bands if the names scrawled on her pencil case are anything to go by.

"He's Number Five on the rock star rich list," I say, "according to your comic".

"This is the NME," Nikki harrumphs.

"Well, whatever it is," I say, "they reckon he's worth over 800 million quid."

"Like I said, some people like him..." Nikki obviously doesn't realise what I'm getting at, and tries to turn the page.

"But that's more money than anybody could spend in a life-time!" I do my best to sound incredulous. Incredulous is a great word, it was in a book we read with Mrs Verity last year.

"I'd give it a go, like," Nikki chuckles.

"Eh?"

"I'd give it a go – spending 800 million – I bet I could find something to spend it on!"

"I'm being serious," I say.

"Ok," she says, closing the magazine and sighing. "What are you getting at?"

"Well, what does he need all that money for?" This is what I'm getting at – it's taken me a while, but Nikki is listening to me now. "Why does he keep writing songs and singing them?"

"Maybe," and I can see her thinking about her answer, "maybe he just enjoys his job".

"But he could retire".

"Maybe he doesn't want to – maybe he'd get bored, maybe he thinks he's so brilliant the world would stop without him!" I can't work out if she's being funny with me, so I carry on.

"But he could give some of it away. He could donate every penny he makes from now on to people who need it – he doesn't need to make anymore for himself". Nikki frowns. "Think about it," I go on "he was at that big concert, you know the one – they raised over fifty million quid for starving people in Africa."

"Yeah," nods Nikki, "I've heard about it".

"Well, just think, if Johnny Marsden had given just one tenth of what he's worth, the starving people would have had eighty million quid and nobody else would have had to lift a finger!" Nikki chews this over for a moment and then says;

"But people wanted to help – people wanted to donate – nobody forced them," she takes a sip from her Ribena carton, "even you give some dosh to charity don't you?"

"Yeah," I say, "of course I do – they got a weeks pocket money out of me".

"Really?" Nikki laughs. "I only gave them half of mine!"

"Well think about that – you gave them half of what you had for a week! Why didn't all of the pop stars at that concert hand over half of what they made in a week? I bet they could've raised more than we did! And I bet they wouldn't be short of cash after they did that!" I'd had to walk into town the week I gave my pocket money to charity – I didn't even save myself the bus fare.

"Yes, but," Nikki trails off, "its not as simple as that... and anyway, doesn't Johnny Marsden do lots of stuff for Cancer charities? And how do you know he doesn't give loads of cash away – people don't have to tell you all about it?"

"He could set a good example – if he told everyone more about it."

"Maybe that's why he did the charity concerts. So that people would think about the issues as well as giving money. Lots of people like his music so maybe he thought that he'd get lots of people to take notice and give money if he was at the concert."

"Ok – so they could've had the concert – but they didn't need to take our money, they could've made us aware and sorted it all out themselves. They didn't have to make me feel so guilty that I gave them all the money I had in the world!"

"Well, I wanted to help as much as I could!"

"So did I! But people are still going hungry – all over the world." I hope I'm not talking too loudly – some of the other kids might think I'm a swot using some of the words

I've been using. "My pocket money is a very small drop in a pretty big ocean – all of them rich people, they could've given some of the money that they'll never have time to spend and a lot more people would've been getting fed!"

"I'm sure they did cough up," she replies.

"But they could all give more. I mean, once they've bought big houses and swimming pools and aeroplanes and stuff, why do they need to keep money in the bank? Why don't they share it out?"

"You can't tell them what to do with their money – people will only do what they can do and even then they'll only do that if they want to. You can't get cross about people who don't do enough – you'll drive yourself crazy."

"If I had that much money I'd give it all away! There are so many good causes, how could you keep it all for yourself? There's people who are ill, who could have better treatment or go abroad for a holiday to cheer them up. How can people not help other people?"

"I'm sure you would give all your money away, but there's no point getting angry because life isn't fair. You can only do what you can do and that's it."

"But people are still homeless and hungry and there are rich people who could be helping without lifting a finger!"

"Why don't you write to them? Maybe you could ask them why they don't give it all away?" I want to tell her that I'm already doing it. I want to tell her about my letters – I want to tell her about how I am trying to make people do more – about how I don't get replies from rich people and powerful people.

"Maybe they think that them singing on a stage is worth more than giving money away."

"Right," Nikki stands up, "I'm finished. I am going to the library to type up my homework – you coming?"

"I haven't had my sandwiches yet," I look down at my lunch. I made it myself. It doesn't look too good, to be honest.

"Well then, you should try shutting up and eating something!" I don't know if she's being serious or if she thinks I'm stupid. Does Nikki agree with me about rich people not helping poor people or doesn't she care? Was she being funny about writing to them? I wonder if we've just had a row.

Damn. What are you supposed to talk about with girls anyway? Music? TV? I see people having these conversations with others, and I wonder what the secret is. Every time I try to have a serious conversation with someone they must think I'm a dick-head.

Reply from the Mayor Number 2

The Office of the Lord Mayor
Town Hall Chambers
21 – 25 Heighington Street

Dear Christopher,

Thank you very much for your letter. I have looked at your suggestions with a great deal of interest, and I will make sure that they are discussed at the next full meeting of the town council.

Yours sincerely

Theresa Rutter (Mrs.)

Letter to the Mayor Number 3

46 Sampson Place
Newton Aycliffe
County Durham

Dear Mrs. Rutter,

It's been on the local news again about young people causing trouble in our town. I wonder if you or your fellow councillors have had a chance to look at my ideas yet? I hope so.

Anyway, the reason I'm writing to you today is because of the bad behaviour of some of the pupils at my school. I hope you'll be interested in some of the things that I've noticed.

Like all schools, we have some people who cause a lot of problems – the teachers call them 'challenging'. Some of the same people behave badly around the town. These pupils have been known to bully others, swear at teachers and one even tried to set fire to the Deputy Head-Teacher's car.

As you would imagine, pupils like this get told off or have letters sent home but in really serious cases, some of them get excluded. Obviously we don't have canes or slippers being used to hit people at school anymore, but I'm afraid some of my fellow pupils don't see being excluded as a punishment. In fact, some of them are doing it deliberately. For example, if one pupil is excluded for two or three days, his/her friends deliberately try to get themselves excluded as well so that they can hang around together while they are off school. Only last week, a female pupil shook up a bottle of pop and opened it in a science lesson just so that she would be excluded at the same time as her friend (who had been excluded earlier in the day for stealing the keys to the food technology cupboard).

I am even more worried by the pupils who want to be excluded permanently. Some of them have heard that if they do something really bad then they will be sent to a special school that is more like a holiday camp. They've heard that they will still do their exams - but in small classes of three of four people. They've also been told that they only have to work in the morning, and in the afternoon they are taken out to do activities like going bowling, rock-climbing or motor-biking. They've even been to concerts and football matches! For most people in my school, who can't afford to pay for such things, this looks like a very good deal. It seems very strange that pupils who behave badly are getting rewarded.

So, I have had an idea! Why don't you offer the same sort of rewards for pupils who behave well at school? Many pupils have good attendance, never get into trouble and always try their best – but they never get noticed. It would even be nice for some of those pupils to be taught in smaller groups and get more help from their teachers – just like the naughty kids do! I'm sure that there are many pupils in my school who would love to go bowling or canoeing or go to see a concert. It would also stop people deliberately trying to get excluded just so that they can have some nice days out.

Please let me know what you think about my ideas. If you like, I could even come to your next council meeting and talk to all of you about them.

Yours sincerely,
Christopher Mason

Tuesday

Mam and nanna have fallen out. Mam told nanna not to bother coming back anymore. She told her that she can manage the house-work by herself, but I know the real reason. She thinks nanna has been going through her things.

"I always leave the drawers of the dresser slightly out," my mam said, "and after your Nanna had been in here, they were pushed too far in! She must've been looking through them!" I suddenly realised that my mam must have been deliberately setting a trap! She doesn't trust any of us!

I kept out of their argument. It always ends with shouting and then my nanna goes home. Eventually, I have to go round to the phone box ring her up and ask her to come back so that my mam isn't on her own when I go to school. Neither of them apologise or talk about the argument. They just behave as though nothing has happened. It's like a cycle they've gotten into. The worst one I ever heard was when they were arguing over Auntie Pat.

"She was always your favourite!"

"Don't talk such bally nonsense!"

"She went to the grammar school and I didn't!"

"I could only afford one uniform!"

"So why did she get it?" And it goes on and on and on. They argue and fight about things that happened before I was even born. I've thought about telling them that it's pretty pointless to rake up the past – I mean, what can either of them do about it? It's gone. Even I'd do stuff differently if I had the chance, and I haven't lived anywhere near as long as them two.

Nobody has taken anything out of the freezer to defrost so I have to go to the fish and chip shop for our tea. I hate it. I don't mind the greasy food, but I have to walk down the main-road and through the estate to get to the chippy. It's awful – especially after dark. There isn't anybody about, and that seems to make it worse. There could be anybody hiding behind the dark fences or lurking in the bushes. The street lights are few and far between and most of the bulbs have gone anyway. I wonder how many of the kids from my school get sent out in the dark to get food for their mam?

The chip shop is busy as usual. The windows are all misted up and the lights are too bright – they've painted the walls white so it looks clean. There's a kid holding his dad's hand in the queue. They don't say anything to each other – they just stand there holding hands. I wonder if the kid will remember this. I wonder if at some point in the future, when him and his dad have a fight or aren't speaking to each other, he'll remember the time he was happy to stand and hold hands with him in the chip shop. I don't remember doing anything nice with my dad.

As I walk home, the parcel of chips is warm underneath my arm. The grease might soak through the chip wrapping and stain the sleeve of my coat. It's another clear night, and I can see right across the estate and out towards the motorway. I can just see the lights of the industrial estate on the far side of the town. There's a big cluster of orangey lights. It looks beautiful – like a galaxy of stars all close together – burning brightly in the night sky. I think it's a battery factory or the sewage works.

"We can manage," my mam always says after my nanna leaves in a huff, but we both know we can't. I tried to cheer her up by asking about when we're going to put the Christmas decorations up this year, but she just shrugged her shoulders. "I don't know if we should bother this year. Nobody ever visits. There's not much point if it's just the two of us." We still haven't heard from my brother.

"Oh," I said, "OK." I'll ask her again in a few days time.

The last time my brother came home things were a bit weird. For one thing, he'd started smoking – which is something I thought I'd never see. My mam has always hated smoking and would never let anybody smoke in the house. She said that it makes the ceiling go yellow. But when my brother came home she said he could smoke upstairs. I was shocked. For one thing, I don't know how he can afford to buy cigarettes because my mam's always telling me that he can't afford to come home because he doesn't have the money for bus fare – but the worst thing was he came into my room and started smoking in there! I wanted to say that I didn't want my clothes and stuff smelling but he didn't seem to think that I cared. He'd changed a lot since before he went to University. He'd started wearing hats and long coats. I think he'd even started wearing nail varnish.

I've noticed that some of my stuff has been moved about in my room. My writing paper is all messed up as if somebody's been looking through it. Maybe my mam is right about my nanna. I hope she didn't read the letters I've been trying to write to Nikki!

Looking For Atlantis

Letter to the Vicar

46 Sampson Place
Newton Aycliffe
County Durham

Dear Mr. Martins,

I hope you don't mind me writing to you, but I do think of myself as part of your congregation even though I don't come to church that often. My mam only ever brings me on Christmas Eve – the rest of the year she is very tired or has a migraine. Both my mam and I have the same problem in that we don't like going places on our own, so if she isn't very well I can't really come along without her,

Anyway, the times I have seen you, you seem like a very nice person, and you often talk about how important love is, and how we need to take care of each other. I think the world would be a much better place if everybody loved each other like you tell them to. After all, Jesus loved all of us so much that he was prepared to die for us, so I suppose he set you a really good example.

My nanna and I often walk past your church onto the way into town, and we always admire the fantastic garden and rose bushes that you have outside the vicarage. It must be brilliant living so close to where you work. I have to walk for twenty minutes every morning just to get to school – and I don't even get paid to go there! Anyway, the Vicarage looks like a very large house (my nanna says it must have four or five bedrooms!) and since your children are grown up, only you and your wife live there. I suppose you must have a lot of empty space nowadays, and it might be nice if you could share your good fortune with others.

As I'm sure you're aware, there are many homeless people in our country – and even in a small town like ours, we have a man who sells the Big Issue outside of the closed-down Woolworths. He seems like a nice man (he's called Tony) and I often think of him at this time of year when the weather is bad and we have a lot of rain. It might be an idea if you could let Tony have one of the empty bedrooms in your house. I'm sure he'd be grateful. It would be a fantastic way to help him – as you wouldn't actually have to give him any money (my nanna says that you shouldn't give money to homeless people as they're all on drink or drugs). It's not as if you'd have to buy a new bed or sheets for him – he's probably used to sleeping in shop doorways or alley-ways so an empty room in your house would seem like the Ritz to him. He'd be out most of the day selling his magazines – he just looks as if he needs somewhere warm where he can get a decent rest. I'd offer to take him in, but we only have a two-bedroomed house.

There must be lots of other vicars (with vicarages) in our County – so please could you mention my idea to them? If they have spare rooms they could take homeless people in, too. Perhaps you could be like Jesus and set a brilliant example for everyone to follow.

If you let me know when Tony can move in, I can give him your address.
Many thanks

Christopher Mason

Looking For Atlantis

Wednesday

David's face isn't so much like thunder it's more like a full-on storm with thunder, lightning, flash-floods and dead bodies floating about.

"Your bloody girl-friend wants locking up!"

He's been trying to change stuff at school again, and as usual, it's all gone horribly wrong.

As well as running the underground school magazine, David is a member of the 'School Council'. It's supposed to be a staff/pupil committee who meet up and look at ways to improve the school. In fact, all they do is organise the end of year trips and Christmas Parties. David has different ideas. At his very first council meeting, he proposed that they should have a vote (involving all staff, pupils and parents) about whether or not the school should continue to have a uniform. Needless to say, Mr. Block (the only teacher who never misses a school council meeting) laughed at him. They did decide to have a non-uniform *day* to raise money for an end of term trip but David was furious. He always gets furious when people don't take him seriously.

So far, David has suggested; a school recycling project (which Mr. Block said was 'too much hassle and a safety hazard'), a school magazine (which they wouldn't allow unless David did all the work but gave Mr. Block total editorial control), and democratic elections for the school council (because David says he is sick of people being allowed to make big decisions just because they're the only ones who can be bothered to turn up for the meetings).

Today was particularly pointless.

"I reckon we should get rid of the vending machines," David said, "they're full of chocolate, crisps and sugary drinks. People are always going on about how obese kids are nowadays, so I think we should do something about it!" I went along to today's meeting because it's a good place to go if it's raining at lunch-time. I even persuaded Nikki to come along.

"Fair enough," said Janice (*'her ladyship'*), who Mr. Block has appointed chair-person of the council because she always does as she's told. "Does anybody second this motion?" She looked around the room. Even though it was raining outside, there were still less than ten people in the room. David looked at me, so I put my hand up. I didn't really want to get rid of the machines – I've often gone and bought a couple of Yorkie bars after a particularly bad P.E. lesson. "That's seconded – we'll have to have a vote."

"Can I just point out," Mr. Block cut in, "that those vending machines are a very important part of school life? For one thing – pupils who want sweets or drinks will always get their hands on them somewhere – and if we get rid of the machines it will mean that more pupils will leave the premises to visit shops, which will undoubtedly lead to increased disturbances in the local community." David shook his head;

"But having those machines in school means that people can get their hands on sweets all day every day. It's not just break or lunch-time! They'll eat and drink loads more crap if it's freely available!" Mr. Block completely ignored him.

"The other important thing to remember is that the company who provides those machines pays this school a great deal of money in order to have them here. Now, we use that money to help fund Christmas parties and end of term activities. If we lose the vending machines, we will have to lose the benefits of having them on the premises." You could see that this had pretty much blown David's argument out of the water. Without their parties and activities to organise the council members wouldn't have anything to feel important about.

David looked really fed up.

"Well, what about taking some of the really unhealthy stuff out of the machines? Can't we have sugar free and caffeine free drinks – and healthy stuff like fruit instead of chocolate and crisps?" I must admit, everybody did look quite thoughtful and David must've thought he was about to achieve something at long last.

"But nobody's going to buy apples and bananas out of a machine!" Nikki snorted as she said this. Everybody turned to look at her, which made me feel really uncomfortable, as I was sitting right next to her. "You aren't going to fool people into buying fruit just because it's in the machine that used to have chocolate in it."

"People need help to make the *right* decisions..." David said.

"But you can't tell people what they can and can't have! People know what's unhealthy – but they don't care because it tastes nice. They've always had the freedom to *choose* what they want to eat, and if you take that away they'll just go somewhere else for their sweets and you'll be left with an awful lot of rotting fruit!" Nikki sounded really cross. She'd sat and listened in silence throughout the meeting, but once she'd started, she'd *really* let fly at David. It was almost as if 'The Bad Dog' had turned up to ruin his lunch-time.

David didn't say anything else for the rest of the meeting. He knew it was pointless. Why would Janice or Mr. Block bother to change anything if they could quite happily find a reason for leaving things exactly as they were?

"I always knew democracy was a rubbish way to get things done," David said as we left the meeting. Nikki is clever, maybe too clever to want to go out with me.

Letter to Nikki – attempt number 31

Dear Nikki,

I'll probably never send this letter. I just haven't got the guts to do it, I suppose. The thing is, I've really enjoyed getting to know you and talking to you at school. I think it's great that we walk home together and we had a brilliant time on the Geography trip (there's no-one I'd rather fall over with!) but I've been absolutely dying to say something to you.

It's funny because since I first spoke to you in that English lesson (you know the one where we had to work in groups) I've felt as though I've known you for a long time. There's just something really familiar about you – almost like we're related or something. You must think I'm a right loony or a freak or whatever, but I'm trying to tell you how I feel. I think I love you. I know that sounds mad coming from a teenager who's only known you a couple of weeks but I've never felt like this about anybody before. I just love talking to you and we make each other laugh and I'd really like to spend more time with you and get to know you better.

I don't know – I've never asked anybody out on a date before. I don't know many places we could go. There's that little café in the town, but it doesn't look very nice. We could go to the pictures in Darlington but you'd probably have to pay your own bus fare because I don't get much pocket money. I suppose I could save up and we could go out once a month or something.

Bloody hell this sounds ridiculous. If I got a letter like this I'd run a mile. But what am I supposed to say? How do you send someone a letter asking them out?

Do I set it out like a multiple choice question?

Nikki – Do you like me as:
A) A friend

B) Potential boy-friend material
C) A bit of a loser?

Should I tell her exactly how I feel? I mean, if I tell her I love her it could scare her off. Saying 'I like you', doesn't really do it justice. Lots of people like lots of things, but it doesn't mean they feel about them the way I feel about her. I could send her a tape with some songs on – 'If You Don't Love Me', 'Cruel', 'We Let The Stars Go'... Maybe I could let Prefab Sprout say it better. But she might not realise what I was on about and just think I'm creepy.

I could've hoovered the stairs and the landing in the time it's taken me to write this load of old crap. And I've still got home-work to do.

Geography on Tuesday

School has been horrible. It's like everybody is getting wound up about the exams and Christmas coming up and everything. David keeps asking me where my wife is, just because I walk to and from school with Nikki every day. He's probably jealous.

On Tuesday, there was a fight in our Geography lesson. Well, it wasn't *really* a fight. Brian accused Mackie of being a Gypsy because his family are living in a caravan (they're having an extension built so it's only a temporary thing, anyway) but Mackie didn't think it was funny. Some people really don't appreciate Brian's sense of humour. Everybody knew he was on thin ice. Mackie has a reputation. Mrs. Nixon once said that he's got a 'fiery temper' just because he has red hair. I asked her why David didn't have a fiery temper but she just gave me one of her looks.

"Say that again," Mackie had hissed across the classroom, "and I'll deck you." Of course, Brian said it again. He actually finds it funny when people get more and more worked up.

"Does your mam sell pegs as well?" Brian looked around, like he always does, waiting for everyone to laugh and think he's wonderful. You could actually hear everybody in the room breathe in suddenly. The last thing you should ever say to Mackie is something nasty about his mam.

Mackie waited until McPherson was in his stock cupboard – then he got out of his seat, walked over to Brian, and punched him in the face. He caught him completely off-guard. Brian was still laughing when the punching began. Mackie punched him again and again and again.

"Don't you ever, ever, ever..." Mackie swore as he punched him. There was blood on his fists by the time he finished. Brian fell on the floor and didn't say anything else.

Mackie went back to his seat and carried on with his work, his hands shaking. A really strange silence fell over the class. Nobody tried to help Brian. Nobody said anything.

When McPherson came out of the cupboard he just stood there, and then put his hands up to his face – he looked like that painting of a man screaming. He didn't say anything. He just walked out of the room.

One of the maths teachers came in to sit with us while Brian was taken away.

"What happened?" We were all asked this by about three different members of staff, including Mr. Block. Nobody said anything. We were threatened with detentions and letters home but everybody kept quiet. We all knew that Mackie would smack any one of us that said anything. It was obvious what had happened. Mackie was sat there, still furious – his head an angry red lump. But the teachers did nothing. Brian hasn't been in school since.

"As if anyone's gonna grass," Nikki said on the way home.

"I know, teachers just don't get it."

"It's a bit mad, though – what happened – and everyone just sat there!"

"Everybody knows that Mackie's a nutter."

"I'm not surprised he hit him!" Nikki said. "Brian deserved it for what he said!"

"What? You mean Mackie was right to hit him because he said something about his mam?"

"No – Brian was being racist – if McPherson had heard they could've chucked him out for that!"

"He only said his mam was selling pegs!"

"He was calling him a Gypsy and using stereotypical ideas that people have about travellers…" Nikki went in to a long story about why Brian had been out of order.

"I don't think he was being racist – he was just being daft!"

"Racists *are* ignorant," Nikki agreed, "either way, he should be in trouble for saying it."

"I can't see Brian as a racist. I've never heard him say anything like that before. And he loves rap music." Nikki just laughed when I said that. Maybe she thinks I'm ignorant, too. "Mackie's the one who should be in trouble – and I'm sure he didn't thump Bri for being a racist – he thumped him because he didn't know how else to shut him up!"

We walked the rest of the way in silence. We both said '*see you tomorrow*' when we got to Nikki's house, but it wasn't the same. I felt the same way as when we talked about rich pop stars – I thought we might be having a row and I don't want Nikki to think that we don't agree about things.

I was going to tell her that I like her after school. And I mean, I was going to tell her that I *really* like her – not just in a friend way – but after what had happened I didn't feel like it.

Looking For Atlantis

Letter to that rich writer bloke

46 Sampson Place
Newton Aycliffe
County Durham

Dear Mr Winters,

May I just say that you are my favourite writer. I read a lot of books (and not just the ones that we do at school) and your novels about the secret time-bending powers of Timothy Clarke are brilliant. I have to keep taking them back to the library to get re-stamped so I can read them over and over again. I also enjoyed the first film that the BBC put on at Christmas (apart from that posh kid who plays Timothy's best friend – he just doesn't seem right).

Anyway, my last two letters must've gotten lost in the post as I never received your reply – maybe your replies got lost! I shall speak to the postman about that in the morning. I think I told you that my mam isn't very well. She has a disease that means her muscles have all stopped working and she can't walk about anymore. She stays in bed most of the time and my nanna comes to help in the house but sometimes they don't get on.

My Mam is getting more poorly every day and she keeps talking about her sister in Australia. It's her twin sister and she emigrated with her family nearly fifteen years ago. They haven't seen each other since and I would like my Mam to go and visit her, because it would be brilliant. I think the nicer weather would probably help her to feel better as well.

My Dad doesn't live with us anymore (just like in the Timothy Clarke stories!) and my Mam has to have Benefits for her money which means we can't afford to go to Australia. I hate to ask you, but I am your biggest fan (I wrote a glowing review of 'Timothy Clarke and Ticking Clocks of Time-world' for my school magazine!) and it said in the paper that you now earn more money than the Queen. Do you think it would be possible for you to loan us the cost of two flights to Australia? I promise I will pay you back when I am older (I am going to be a writer! Guess who inspired me!) and it would mean the world to my Mam. I know you used to be poor yourself and I hope you remember how people helped you back then.

Your biggest fan

Christopher Mason

Looking For Atlantis

Thursday Evening

I really don't know what I'm going to say. I've got my little bag of coins and the hand-set is in my hand, but I really don't know what I'm going to say.

There's never a queue at the phone-box anymore. Everybody must have phones at home or mobiles. Mind you, that hasn't stopped them kicking the glass out of this one. And it smells like people use it for a loo on their way home from the pub.

If I was sure about how I feel, I wouldn't be hesitating, would I? I mean, if I was 100% sure of myself I would just call her up and tell her. But what the hell am I supposed to say?

'I like you, do you like me?'

'Will you go out with me?'

'Do you want to go the pictures?'

That all just sounds like bollocks to me. Should I try to be funny, should I take the mickey out of myself? Or should I be confident and just assume that she feels the same way? How do other people know how to do this? I don't have a dad to ask for advice and my older brother doesn't seem to be the sort of older brother who would be very helpful anyway. He'd probably say something sarcastic if I asked him.

Bloody hell. They don't really cover this bit in pop songs. Failed romances, dead lovers, nights of passion – everybody writes songs about that! Why can't somebody write a song about how to ask someone out?

I dial her number. It rings. For a second I have hope. Maybe nobody will answer, or maybe it'll be an answer-machine – then I can go home and live in hope for a bit longer. No such luck.

"Hello?" It's a male voice. Brother? Dad?

"H-h-hello," I must sound like a moron. "Could I have Nikki please?"

"Excuse me?" It must be her dad, he sounds unhappy and grown-up.

"Erm, d-does Nikki live there?"

"She does, yes."

"Could I speak to her, please?"

"Who shall I say is calling?"

"Erm, well just say it's Chris from school."

"OK Chris from school – one moment." He puts the receiver down and I can hear him shouting up the stairs to Nikki. I could still put the phone down. I could deny that I rang. I could say it was kids from school trying to wind her up. It's not too late. I can still run away.

"Hello, Chris?" It's her! Bugger.

"Hi, Nikki, I ..erm, I ..erm, I ..erm"

"Are you OK?"

"I'm fine, yes."

"I'm glad you rang," she says. What does she mean by that? Has she been waiting for me to call? Has she been going through the same thing?

"R-really?"

"Yeah – that English home-work is a nightmare – I just can't stand poetry." So she wanted my help! She needs me!

"Oh, OK – well I needed to speak to you. It's something that's been on my mind for a while." I have to get these words out. This might be the only chance that I have. I don't know if I'll ever get this far into a conversation with her ever again.

"We only got the home-work today."

"It's not the home-work – it's about me and you."

"Eh?"

"Well, people have been saying stuff about me and you at school."

"Like what?"

"Stuff," I say, and take a deep breath. "People have been talking about how we walk home together and how we have lunch together and sit together in lessons, and…"

"Oh, I know," she says, "they're a bunch of immature idiots. They think just because we spend time together that we must be going out with each other."

"Yes!" I blurt out. "They think we're in love or something."

"Ha!" Nikki laughs. Nikki *laughs*. "They really need to grow up – they live in a world where men and women just can't be friends. Jesus – they need to get a life!"

"So you're not upset…" I'm not sure this is going where I want it to go.

"Oh no – Christ – let the little kids say what they want. It doesn't change the fact that you're my best mate!"

"Yeah." I'm her best mate. I don't want to be her best mate. "I mean, it's not like we really are going out…"

"Exactly!" She sounds happy. "I'm just glad that we're more mature than the rest of the dick-heads in our school. I don't know how I'd have survived without you these last few weeks!"

"Right, yeah, me too – I mean – I'm glad I've got you, too." I actually feel sick.

"So anyway," she says, "this Wordsworth thing…"

"Can we do it at break or dinner tomorrow?" I rush the words out – I just want to get off the phone now and go home. "I'm in a phone-box and I haven't got much change left…" I actually have plenty of tens and twenties left.

"Oh, OK – well, see you tomorrow!"

"Yeah, bye." Click, thunk – dialling tone. She's gone. She's off the line. I pick up my bag of coins.

I need to go home. I need to lie down and put my headphones on and I need to listen to some Prefab Sprout. I need to hear that song about falling in love with your best friend. I don't know how I should feel right now. Shouldn't I be glad that I've got this brilliant best friend who I can talk to and spend time with? I don't know.

I've got quite a good idea for a new 'Black Dog' comic strip.

Looking For Atlantis

Letter to *** (can't bring myself to write it)

I know that is completely out of the blue, but I need to talk to you.
I will be able to come through to South Shields on a Saturday if that's OK.
I don't want my mam to know that I'm coming to see you, but there are a lot of things I need to talk to you about.

I can meet you at the café opposite the museum (if it's still there) at two o'clock in the afternoon.

We don't have a phone at the moment – so if you can't make it, then I'm sorry but you will have to write to me.

Please don't use your own handwriting on the envelope as my mam will recognise it and she won't be happy.

Christopher.

Friday Morning

"The way I see it," says David, "is that they can afford to lose that money." We're sitting in the Art room and David is telling me all about his plan. We have another still life in front of us. This time, it's an old shoe and an empty crisp packet. Mr. Mowatt must really want to stretch our talent. "They've made a fortune by exploiting others…" He must see the puzzled look on my face. "I mean, they sell sweets and sugary crap that make people fat – no offence – "

"None taken."

"- So really, they should *have* to pay something back." We can talk like this in Art because Mr. Mowatt is busy helping Janice to finish off a pot she's been trying to make.. "Cigarettes get taxed because they're unhealthy, so it's about time some-one taxed the sweets and crisps a little bit." David has obviously got this all worked out in his head. I'm not convinced.

"But what are you going to do? You can't just tell them to do it - write them a letter and tell them about your idea – see how far you get!"

"Exactly! I *did* write a letter to the Prime Minister *and* the Chancellor of the Exchequer and neither of them wrote back! I think we'll have to act *ourselves*." I want to ask David if he actually did write to them. I never thought of writing to the Chancellor of the whatsit. "And we could get something done about those vending machines at the same time." David is still sore about the school council meeting. I almost feel guilty, because if it wasn't for me, Nikki would never have been there.

"David – what can you actually do? We're kids – we're school kids, and I'm pretty sure nobody gives a toss what we think." I'm sick of wasting my time on writing letters and I'm sick of spending money on stamps.

"We hit them where it hurts!" David kicks the bag that he has under his chair. It gives off a loud metal clang.

"Eh?"

"It's a crow-bar!"

"What, you're going to beat up the vending machines?"

"Don't be soft. We're going to break *into* the machines. We're going to take the money that they're making and we're going to give it to charity!"

"That's not going to work!"

"Of course it is. We stay behind for a revision class, and after they think everybody's gone home, we lever the cash boxes open on all the machines. There'll be a fortune sitting in them at the end of the day. And you can guarantee – as soon as the machines stop making money, the companies that provide them will take them out of the school." David must think he's Robin Hood.

"That's stealing, David. You'd get caught."

"No we wouldn't – because one of us acts as a look-out! And anyway – it's only wrong if you look at it from a certain point of view."

"Well the Police would probably look at it that way."

"In a way, we're doing people a big favour by getting rid of the machines and giving a load of money to charity. How can that be wrong? It's not like we'd be keeping the money for ourselves." David keeps saying 'we' and 'our' like he assumes I'm going to agree and help him out. "As long as we tell ourselves that it's the right thing to do, then we won't have a problem."

"We'll end up in that school for bad kids on the outskirts of town."

"I've told you – it's not gonna happen."

It's an idea. Maybe I should tell David about my mam and ask him if he thinks we could 'find' enough money to send her to Australia. The only real problem I can see is that all of the money is going to be in coins. Tens, twenty and fifty pieces are all those machines take. If we're lucky we might find a few pound coins – but it's going to look a bit odd buying plane tickets with bags full of small change. I'm sure Tony the homeless guy won't mind if we give him a load of change, but they'll think we're weird at the Travel Agents.

"You two!" Mowatt is finally taking notice of his class. He must've finished with Janice's pot by now. "Get on with it!" He stands behind us and looks at our work. "You're a hopeless case, lad," he says to David, "the way you've drawn it, that shoe must belong to the Elephant Man."

Letter to the croaky voiced singer

46 Sampson Place
Newton Aycliffe
County Durham

Dear Steve Wilton,

Hi Steve – I realise you probably get a lot of fan letters – but this one is different. You see, I'm writing on behalf of my mam. She thinks you're the best singer she's heard since Bryan Adams and she wanted to vote for you on that Pop talent show thing but we haven't got the phone at the moment. She thought you were amazing when you did 'Run to You' and that song off the Robin Hood film so I've promised to get her your CD single for her birthday.

Anyway, I was reading on teletext about the hard life you had before you won the TV show. It said that your Mam was really ill and that she had inspired you to give your best performances in the competition. That's such a coincidence Steve, because my Mam is ill, too! And your singing has really made a difference to her – every Saturday night she really seemed to brighten up when you sang on the TV. My Mam is getting more poorly so it's good that you cheered her up – and I'm trying to make things even better for her. My Mam has a twin sister who lives in Australia and they haven't seen each other for over ten years! My Mam has always wanted to go over and see her but because we are on benefits it looks as though we'll never get the chance. We've been asking our family and friends if they can help us to raise the money – maybe you have some good ideas about how we could do that?

It would be really nice to hear from you Steve, I'm sure my Mam would be thrilled if she got a letter with your autograph on or something.

Yours sincerely

Christopher Mason

Looking For Atlantis

Friday Afternoon

I've failed that one. I must have.

I wonder if it really counts as a fail if I didn't even get around to putting my name on the paper. It's not as if I couldn't have answered some of the questions, or tried to show some of my working out – I just couldn't see the point. Maths is crap anyway. All of the maths teachers are boring and miserable – which must prove something.

I've just sat in a two hour exam and done absolutely nothing. I didn't write on the desk, I didn't doodle on the back of the exam paper – I sat there staring into space. And nobody noticed. We had teachers wandering around, handing out rulers, pencils and calculators – and not one of them stopped to ask me why I hadn't started answering the questions. It wasn't even a proper exam in the school hall. We were just in a class-room. The teachers probably just wanted an easy lesson. They know we'll all shut up if it's supposed to be an exam. The only noise was the turning of papers and the foot-steps of teachers. Every now and again somebody would drop a pen or a ruler and you'd hear a member of staff tut or speed up their feet so they could tell someone off. Nobody bothered me.

I actually sat and ran through my own personal 'Best of Prefab Sprout' in my head. I've listened to their stuff so often, I really do know all the words. I thought I'd start with something upbeat (but still melancholy!) like 'A Prisoner of the Past' and then move through the real heartbreaking stuff like 'Bonny', 'Appetite' and '*When Love Breaks Down*'. And I had to put '*Goodbye Lucille #1*' in there because it has the best line ever;

"Life's not complete 'til your heart's missed a beat".

I wonder if my life's complete now, then?

By the end of the exam I had about twenty tracks in the order that I'd put them on my compilation tape. I might put it together when I get home. I'm surprised nobody saw my lips moving as I tried to remember some of the words. The exam paper stayed shut and I didn't even bother getting my pencil case out.

Here's why:

I spent lunch-time with Nikki as usual – and it seemed just like a regular day. I even managed to eat some of my sandwiches in front of her! I did wonder if she'd noticed that I'd lost a bit of weight recently. Not eating and not sleeping were certainly having a bit of an effect. We talked about music and the telly, and I realised that I am actually starting to get my head round having conversations and being able to chat to people. We had the usual clanking noises and messy tables, but I was feeling pretty good.

"What are you doing over the weekend?" I can't believe I actually asked her that. It just sort of came out. We were talking about what a git McPherson is for giving us home-work when he knows we've got exams to revise for – and it just sort of happened. I asked her what she was doing over the week-end. I was going to suggest that we go to the town library to do our home-work, maybe even go to the nasty little café in the basement for a cup of tea – but then the world came crashing down all around me.

"Oh this weekend is going to be great!" Nikki's eyes sparkled. "My boyfriend's driving down from Berwick!" I'm not sure which piece of information was more of a kick in the bollocks. Nikki has a boyfriend was a pretty big kick. But Nikki has a boyfriend who is old enough to drive a car was like being kicked by someone wearing steel toe-caps.

"Really?" I felt my throat closing up. I actually did have trouble getting the word out.

Looking For Atlantis

"Yeah! My Dad doesn't really approve because Sal's a little bit older than me – but even *he* said that it's nice of him to drive all the way down here on his day off!"

Here's what I wanted to say;

"You never said you had a boy-friend! (Mind you, you never said that you didn't have a boy-friend.) Do you really think you should be going out with some-one who is at least three years older than you? Is he a safe driver? If he's only getting one day off, does that mean he has a job? How old is he? You could do better!"

Here's what I *actually* said:

"Great. That'll be really great." I wonder if she saw how red my face was. I couldn't eat anymore. My throat was sticky, and I felt as if I was going to stop breathing. I felt as if someone was pressing their fingers down hard on the top of my skull. The end of lunch-time couldn't come quick enough. If it hadn't been for the maths exam I probably would've gone straight home.

My head actually hurts. They never say that in love songs. My head hurts and I feel like I want to close my eyes, but when I close my eyes it just gets worse. I remember being travel sick a long time ago, in the car when I was little – and it's a bit like that, as if I'm too weak to move my arms and legs and my neck can't support my head. Every second seems to last an hour and I just want the world to go away. My stomach feels like I've got a beached whale in there – it's massive and grey and heavy and it doesn't feel like it's ever going to move.

When I came home, after the exam, I didn't wait for Nikki. I didn't even use the short-cut across the school-field and over the bridge. I walked out of the main school gates and all the way round to Burn Lane. Burn Lane is just a massive dip with a road running up and down it. It's a bugger to walk up the other side, and my shins were aching by the time I got to the top. My school bag felt heavier than ever, and it took an extra twenty-five minutes to get home, but I couldn't walk the same way as Nikki.

My mam didn't even notice anything different about me when I got here. She was watching TV.

I changed out of my uniform, put the dry dishes away and then came up to my room.

I'm now sitting amongst the empty sleeves of the Prefab Sprout albums, working out if I've got enough time on a ninety minute cassette for all the songs I want to put on.

I remember the last time my brother came home and he saw that I still had all of the Prefab Sprout albums lying about in my room.

"That's so boring," he said, "are you really still listening to all of this old stuff? It'd bore me to tears." As soon as he went to University everything at home became boring. I tried to tell him about the books we were reading at school and about how since Woolworths shut the only place to get music nowadays is in the town library. He just kept saying: "that library is so tiny – they don't have much worth reading – how can you keep listening to the same few songs over and over again?" He sat on the floor in my bedroom, smoking cigarettes and looking through the books I had to read for school.

"God I remember this one – it was so boring…"

Even when we went down to the town centre so that he could help me carry the shopping he kept talking about how dull everything was. We went to the newsagents where we used to buy pens and books and stuff and he said he couldn't believe how small it was and that he used to be so bored going around the little town centre every week.

I'm half way through side b of my tape and I've still got two more albums to pick songs from.

Looking For Atlantis

Yet Another letter To Auntie Pat

46 Sampson Place
Newton Aycliffe
County Durham

Dear Auntie Pat,

I'm starting to get worried because we haven't heard from you for ages and ages. I hope you've been getting my letters and I hope something horrible hasn't happened to any of you.

Actually, in some ways, it might be better if something has happened to you and you can't reply because you've been in an accident or you're ill. Maybe you're too busy to write back to your family in England, I don't know, but I think that's a real shame if you are.

Families should stick together – especially when times are bad, but I feel as if you don't really want to know about mam and how ill she is. She gets dead miserable because she can't leave the house, you know, and it would really cheer her up just to get a letter from you.

I had hoped you might offer to pay for her flights over to see you, but nanna says that it's too expensive. I suppose it's up to you what you spend your money on, but you could at least afford the price of a stamp to send my mam a letter. Maybe Uncle Pete could post it out through his work and save on the postage.

Mam is staying in bed a lot more than she used to – it's almost like she can't see any point in getting up – and I'm dead worried about her.

I'd better go – I won't write again until we hear from you, because I feel a bit silly writing all of these letters and never getting any back.

Love
Chris.

Breaking the law

Chris looks at the letters he's received.

The office of the Prime Minister sent a short letter, thanking him for 'his suggestions' but explaining how busy the life of a Prime Minister is. They didn't do anything.

Chris got a similar letter from the Prince of Wales – a polite reply from somebody who opens the post for an important person.

Chris's 'favourite' author didn't even bother to reply at all. Maybe he only writes what he gets paid to write. And the bank didn't answer. The bank didn't want to help. Nobody wants to help.

So Chris has decided that enough is enough. People don't actually want to help other people – so he's going to have to do something. The people who could help don't care so he's going to have to make his plans alone.

He sits in his room and thinks about the operation carefully. He knows that Friday is delivery day – but that's also the busiest day for customers, too. Chris doesn't want too many people about, just in case some of them cause a scene or try to get involved. First thing Saturday morning is looking like the best time to do it – it's the only time that the banks are open and Chris doesn't have to go to school.

He makes a list of the equipment that he's going to need. A mask is important. The place is full of CCTV cameras and he can't risk being recognised. He's even going to wear three or four jumpers under his coat so that he looks bulkier and more grown up. He's also written a note so that he doesn't have to speak to anybody. People might be able to tell how young he is if he has to speak.

The note is important – he's taken a long time to get the wording right. The note will be read by the Police and it'll probably get published in newspapers or read out on the telly. Apart from asking for the money, Chris has decided that the note should make a statement. He wants the world to know why he's doing this –
"This money is needed by people who can't help themselves."

As long as he stays calm and gets in and out quickly then Chris doesn't see how his plan can fail. As soon as he gets the money and gets out of the door, Chris has worked out that he can duck down behind the wheelie-bins in the alley-way next to the bank. He knows that the bins will be there on Saturday. Monday is bin-man day in the town. He can dump the mask and extra clothes – he's thought about burning them in case the Police can get DNA off them, but what's the point? They won't think to check the DNA against any school kids. He can wander away with the money in a carrier bag – no-one is going to suspect a teenager of anything. Chris has always has good reports and has never been in trouble at school for something he's actually done, so why would anybody even consider him as a suspect?

He'll have the money to take his mam to Australia and the rest is going to charity. In fact, if Chris gets away with it, he's planning to do this sort of thing quite often. Maybe Chris can go on taking money from banks and building societies and then he could donate more and more to people who really need it. He could give money to the Big Issue seller outside of Woolworths and he could post envelopes stuffed with cash through the letter-boxes of every charity shop in town. He could help everybody who needed helping. But he'd have to be careful. He'd have to make sure that he didn't keep anything for himself. Chris doesn't want money. To him, it seems that people who do have vast amounts of money don't actually help others as much as poor people do.

He walks into the bank, his coat buttoned up to the top, and his hood up. He's wearing a plastic Frankenstein's monster mask – he's chosen that one because loads of people seemed to buy them at Halloween – there's nothing rare or unusual about it. He doesn't wait in the queue – he pushes in front of the other customers and slides his note under the glass partition. The bank teller frowns as she reads it, then looks up at him. He sees the confusion and the fear in her eyes. He can't avoid scaring people, but it won't last long. The woman fills a bag with money – she's obviously been trained not to do anything reckless – and she slides it through the window. Chris grabs the bag and walks slowly out of the bank. The other customers sit on the floor, terrified and hopeful at the same time. They know they've all done the sensible thing. Nobody has tried to be a hero. Nobody has tried to interfere. Nobody has been hurt. Chris didn't even have to show anybody the replica gun that he bought at the indoor market. It only fires brightly coloured pellets, but from a distance nobody would know the difference.

If it all does go wrong, Chris has a slightly different plan. If the Police arrive or if he gets caught, then he'll tell the world how he was driven to desperate measures in order to help his Mam and all the other people in the world who get ignored and left to fend for themselves. Chris knows that his story will make the front pages and the whole country will express their sympathy for him. Maybe then things will change. As far as Chris can see, if his plan works then it'll be brilliant, and even if it doesn't work, it will still do some good.

Looking For Atlantis

But most of all, Chris knows that apart from planning a trip for his Mam, he's not spending any of the money himself. That would be wrong.

Saturday, meeting with ***

He's a bit balder than I remember him. He still has black hair above his ears and at the back of his head – and he's combed the last few strands from the front backwards – he must have gel or mousse or something on it.

"Do you want a milkshake?" I didn't expect him to have such a strong Geordie accent. I grew up miles from here so I'm not used to hearing people talk like this. I can remember some of the things he said when I was little – but I don't recognise the sound of his voice.

"Um," I think a milk-shake might make me look a kid, "I'll have a cup of tea," then I remember my manners, "please."

"OK," he frowns, and turns to the counter. I'm left standing there – wondering what I should do. He turns to me once more, "d'y'wanna go and sit doon?"

"OK," I say, "Yeah – I'll be over…" I wave my hand towards one of the small booths at the back of the seating area. I wonder how many ice cream parlours there are like this one. This one has been here as long as I can remember. It's one of the few memories I've got from when my mam and him were still together. They brought me here and he'd bought me a book about cartoons and I remember they argued about how much he'd spent on it. And then they had tea while I had a milk-shake. We didn't eat anything and nobody said very much. The colour of the walls is still the same – it's an orangey brown – and the tables still have metal edges and are covered in scratches. My mam and my nanna remember this place. They sometimes talk about living in Shields when mam was younger. My nanna reckons she met the family that started this place up – the first Italian family in South Shields. She said that they don't do all the flavours that they used to because local people didn't like them – but my nanna still remembers the beautiful and exotic flavours that came all the way from Italy. Mind you, my nanna has a lot of stories like that – and she never lets the truth get in the way of a good story.

"So, how's school?" he starts setting the drinks down on our little table. "OK," I shrug, I don't know what else to say about school, to be honest. He sits down and starts stirring sugar into his milky tea. One, two, three sugars – my mam would go mad!

"D'y'get lots of home-work?"

"Yeah." I really feel as though I should be saying more – actually having a conversation instead of just answering questions, "sometimes."

"Y'got plenty of friends?"

"Yeah. Well, some…"

"Y'got a girl-friend?"

"Kind of," I feel myself blushing. If only he knew. I'm scarlet. "Well, she's a girl, and she is my friend." That just about sums her up, I suppose.

"Did'ya watch the match on Sundee?"

"Match?" This isn't what I'd been expecting. This was supposed to be a serious, grown up conversation about serious, grown up stuff!

"The football, on Sky – did'ya watch it on Sundee?"

"Oh, no." I hate football. At least I think I do. I've tried not to watch it – mainly because my mam said he liked it so much. I didn't want to be like him – not in front of her.

"D'ya not watch the footy?" He actually sounds surprised. Why should he be?

"Erm, no, we haven't got Sky, my mam says it's a waste of money."

"Oh." He sits quietly for a while, stirring his tea before taking a sip. It's too hot and he tries to cool it down by blowing on it. We sit there in the little ice cream parlour for a couple of minutes, without speaking. I haven't tried my tea yet. At last he says something else, he says: "I was pleased to get your letter. It was a nice surprise." I had to send it to the Police Station because I don't know where he lives nowadays.

I didn't want to write to him. I don't know much about him. "I was dead proud of you, because it was a proper grown up letter." I'm glad I'm not drinking any tea because I probably would have choked.

"How's ya mam?"

"OK," I reply. But that's not right, I didn't come here to tell him that everything was fine. "Actually – she's not," I blurt out, "she's really bad at the moment".

"Yeah?" his eyebrows arch, "what's up with her?"

"She's ill," I say, "she's really bad – she hardly ever gets out of bed".

"Oh," he says with a sigh, "that sounds like her". How can he know? It's years since *they* lived together.

"What do you mean?"

"Well, ya mam always seemed to have a bad head or something," he looks at me as though I should be nodding in agreement. I don't. "She did, didn't she? She always seemed to need a 'lie down' – she couldn't face this and she couldn't face that…"

"I think this is a bit different." I blow on my tea – it's still so hot that it's burning my hand through the cup!

"Yeah, well – she always needed a lie down if we'd planned to go out somewhere or if my mam and dad were coming to visit. Migraines, she used to say – always bloody migraines."

"No, you don't know what it's like – it's *not* migraines"

"Oh," he says, and I think he might even be sneering – maybe I shouldn't have brought all this up so soon – "so is it her *nerves*, then? That's the other line she always used. She used to have tablets off the doctor for her *nerves*."

"No – it's not her nerves." I can't believe I've come all this way and all he's doing is slagging off my mam – and he doesn't even know what he's talking about! "She's sick – she's really sick. Some days she can't feel her arm – some days she can't feel one whole side of her body – she really is stuck in bed most of the time!" I hope I haven't been shouting. Apart from the staff, we're the only people in here, but I do worry about showing myself up. Especially in front of *him*.

"She's that bad?" I can see it all over his face that he doesn't believe me – not completely. He doesn't trust my mam, so he doesn't trust me when I talk about her.

"I have to take her a cup of tea and some toast before I got to school," I say, "I don't like leaving her on a morning but my Nanna can't get to ours before ten o'clock because of the buses – and my Mam can't do much by herself." He sits and drinks his tea and then pulls a face.

"Sounds like she's got you round her little finger," is all he says.

"What?" I can't actually believe it. My nanna always said he was a 't-u-r-d' (she used to spell it out rather than say it, but now I know what she meant).

"She's got you taking her breakfast in bed every morning because she wants a lie in!" he laughs – he *laughs*. "You and your nanna running around after her! She wants to snap out of that and grow up! My mam always said she was highly strung!" I want to throw my tea in his face. I want to scald his big fat laughing head.

"Look," I say, gripping my tea-cup tight, "she's not going to get better – she's just going to keep on getting worse and worse and worse…"

"Oh come on," he sneers, "she's taken you for - " but he stops then, maybe he's had second thoughts. Maybe he's seen the way I'm holding my tea-cup, maybe he's seen the dark rings around my eyes, maybe he's seen that my clothes haven't been ironed properly – I don't know what it is, but something has gotten to him. "You're serious, aren't you?" he says.

"She's got this thing," I almost choke on the words, "it's wasting her muscles – she can't walk – I have to push her in a wheel-chair just to get some air in the garden. We have to bath her and everything."

"Oh Jesus," he puts his cup down. He looks as though he wants to say sorry, but doesn't.

We sit quietly for a bit. One of the waitresses comes over and wipes down our table. I hate it when they do that – especially when you haven't even finished your drink.

"Why didn't you tell me?" he says at last.

"I just have".

"Why didn't you tell me *before*?" I wonder what difference it would've made. I'd like to ask him what he would've done to help, but instead I say;

"I didn't know where you were".

"Rubbish," he hisses, "your mam has always had my work number! She rang me to tell you about your brother and his A levels."

"She's never given it to me!" I say "she doesn't know I'm here now – she'd probably go crazy if she found out – she *hates* you." I don't feel cruel saying that – not at all – he already knows what she thinks of him.

"So – why are you here, if she doesn't want you to have anything to do with me?"

"I don't know," and I really don't. I'm supposed to be asking him for help, but I kind of always knew that he wouldn't believe me or wouldn't want to help – so why am I here? "I don't know," I say again, "I thought you might know what I could do – how I might help her."

"I don't know what you mean," he says, shuffling in his seat. "I mean, if there was something I could do to help *you*, you know I'd do it. But to be honest, I don't know what I can do."

So we have some more silence. A coffee machine gurgles. Somebody scrapes a cup against a saucer. I look at the bald bits of my dad's head. It suddenly occurs to me that baldness is hereditary.

"Did you know my Auntie Pat?" I ask him.

"Your mam's twin? Of course I knew her. She was a nice girl." He thinks for a moment, "didn't she marry an insurance salesman?"

"Uncle Colin, yeah".

"So they're still together," he says. I nod. "So where's she? Can't she help with your mam?"

"She's in Australia, now. She emigrated with Uncle Colin when I was five." That was about two years after he left.

"Bloody hell," he chuckles, "Little Pat went to Oz! Well, they do say it's a great life out there!"

"Yeah – it is supposed to be great out there," and I know I've got to go for broke – it might be another nine or ten years before I see this bloke again. "Mam always wanted to go out there, to visit Pat – she always said we'd do it!"

"Your mam, on a plane?" he snorts, "that'll be the day – she was scared of crossing the road when I knew her".

"I wrote to Auntie Pat," I do my best to ignore what he's saying – I have to say my piece. "I told her all about what was happening with Mam – I told how she'd always wanted to see Australia – how it would be nice for the pair of them, the twins to see each other again."

"Did she reply?"

"They sent us a post-card," I can tell my voice is wobbling – but I will not cry in front of him. "It had a Koala Bear on it. She didn't even mention my Mam being ill or us going to Australia – she just went on about how lovely and hot it always is – and how well my cousins are doing at school!"

"Aye, well they've got their own lives out there," my Dad nods, "it's hard to know what to say or do for the best"

"I thought," and I almost spit the words out, "that she might've helped".

"What? How could she help if she's in Australia? It's not like she's gonna get a bus each morning, is it?" Then it seems to dawn on him. He seems to realise what I'm getting at. "Is that why you wanted to see *me*?"

"No." What do I say? "I don't know." I try to look him in the eye but he looks away. "Mam has always wanted to go to Australia – it's this big thing about how everything is better over there…"

"*And?*" his voice sounds harder.

"We've never been able to afford it. Mam says we haven't got the money. She only gets benefits."

"Look Chris, what do you expect me to do about that?"

"I thought," and I swallow hard, "that you might help me with the money".

"*What?*" he's embarrassed at how loud he says this and he laughs to cover it up.

"Well, you could lend me the money"

"Chris – we are talking about thousands and thousands of pounds…"

"I know," I go for eye contact again, but he's not having it, "but I'll get a job and I will pay it back"

"And how many paper rounds do you think you'll have to do?"

"This is all she wants," I say, "I'll do it."

"OK," he sighs, "let's just pretend for a moment that I've got the kind of money that you're talking about. Do you honestly think that your Mam would be able to travel? Do you think she could get on a plane? I bet you don't even have passports…"

"I can sort all that out, if we had the money, I'd make sure it was all sorted!"

"Travel companies and airlines have all sorts of rules about sick people," he says, as if he's explaining things to a baby.

"I can do it," I say, "I would be there to look after her and make sure that everything was OK, no travel company or airport or pilot are going to say no to me or my mam – we just need the money!"

"You're living in a bloody fantasy world". He drains the last of his tea. He clanks his spoon into the empty cup.

"Look," I try to reason with him again, "I've never asked you for anything. Never. I *need* to do this."

"And besides," he starts up, as if he hasn't heard what I've just said "what makes you think that I've got that kind of money?" I'm a bit taken aback by this.

"Mam says you're in the Police – quite high up – my nanna says you must be on a good wage by now."

"And I don't get to see much of it," he says, "once the tax-man has his cut, and I still have to pay money to your mam for you."

"Not much," so my mam says, "and you don't have to pay for Rob now he's over eighteen."

"But I still pay what the court says I have to," he grimaces, "and I pay it on time." I open my mouth to reply but he carries on; "and what you don't understand is that I have a life – I have other responsibilities. After me and y'mam split up I got on with my life, y'know. I got married again – settled down – I've got three other bairns that need feeding and clothing!"

"You've got *another family?*" this is news to me.

"Yeah – and the court makes me pay for them, too"

"Oh right," and I realise what he's getting at, "so not only have you been married again, you've been divorced again, too!"

"I've been married three times son. Three marriages, five bairns. It's a lot to take care of." He sees the look on my face. "I work bloody hard for what I've got – and every month a big chunk of my salary goes to four bairns that I never even see!"

"Hang on, you don't see any of your kids?" He shuts up. He looks down. He looks at me.

"It's complicated," is all he says.

"How?" I say, "how is it so complicated that you can't phone or write once in a while?"

"Chris – I have thought about you every single day since I last saw you…" his eyes go misty – is this an act? "I've always wondered about what you were doing and who you were with."

"Why didn't you ask me?"

"It's complicated," he looks down again, and sighs. "When me and your mam stopped living together it was *difficult*." He's trying to pick his words carefully. "We both thought it would be *better* for you, less *unsettling* for you if I wasn't around. You used to get very upset and you have to understand that grown-ups..." he knows that he's patronising me – that's why he stops like this. "I didn't want to hurt you."

"But what about Christmas? And birthdays? Would it have been so difficult to send a card?" I really feel as if I want to shake him and rant at him and spit in his eye. But I stop. My voice tails off.

"I don't know what to say."

"Yeah" I stand up. I have tears welling up in my eyes but I don't want him to see. "Thanks for tea but I have to get going – still have shopping to get – have a bus to catch..." I'm babbling.

"Chris," he says calmly, "sit down, we'll have another cup of tea. I'll run you home, don't worry about that..."

He's trying to sound reasonable but I'm biting back tears. I hurry out of the Ice Cream Parlour, back onto Ocean Road. I wanted to ask him about Prefab Sprout and all of his records. I wanted to know how a man who can like such brilliant songs can turn out to be a total bastard. But I can't stand to be near him for one second longer.

He doesn't try to follow me. He stays there, sitting behind his empty cup.

Looking For Atlantis

A Letter from Rob

Hi Mam!

I'm sorry I haven't been home for a while but they're making us do extra exams in the run up to Christmas. I think they're trying to make sure that we're all kept on our toes for the finals next Summer.

I've got a few essays and a lot of revision to get through so it doesn't look like I'm going to get home for my birthday. I know all of this work will be worth it in the end and I'm sure you'll agree that I have to make some sacrifices in the short term. I don't even think I'll be able to come home for very long at Christmas – we get four weeks holiday but I'm planning on staying through here so I can use the University Library and the computers. Tutors expect all of the work to be typed up nowadays and I can't do that at home.

I've also been rehearsing for a new production that the University Theatre Group is putting on. Fran, the bloke who runs it, says I have real talent as a performer! I only joined to try and get one of my plays put on, but now he wants me to take one of the main roles as well! I never thought anybody would think that I could act. I remember being King Herod in the school nativity but this is something else! I'm very nervous because sometimes they get over forty people in the audience at Theatre Group productions. Fran has said we should all carry on after we graduate next year and go to the Edinburgh festival.

Anyway – I must dash, we're all meeting up in the college bar before rehearsals tonight. I hope you are all well and I'll write again soon.
Love,

Rob

The Next Weekend

It's not much of a view. It's certainly not the one I thought we'd have.

I can see right across the mouth of the river. There's a muddy bank opposite our hotel, and I can see the bridges – all of the bridges. The winter sun is hanging low and there are bright reflections on the windows from the hotels, bars and offices. I only open the window a little bit – I don't want the cold to get in. I didn't realise there were so many hotels in Newcastle and I certainly didn't realise how many shiny new buildings there are. We're quite high up, maybe on the eighth or ninth floor and our room is really nice.

My nanna said that we all need a break from time to time. She paid for and organised all of this. I've told her that I'll pay her back but she said it can wait. She's still not talking to mam, so she told me not to say where I'd got the money from. I told her about the letter we got from Rob and she didn't say anything.

My mam is sleeping. She's not used to such excitement. The staff on the train were very good. They had some bloke in a waist-coat who helped us on and off and made sure we had enough room at our table for the wheel-chair. He asked us if we wanted tea or coffee and even my mam seemed pleased at how well we were treated.

Nanna paid for our taxi to Darlington station, and the tickets were waiting for us. She even gave me some money so that we could get a taxi from Newcastle station to the hotel, even though it's only a five minute trip. We were taken straight to the front of the taxi queue by the man in the waistcoat.

When we got to the hotel it was like getting onto a cruise-ship or something. Just inside the big glass doors they have shiny wooden floors and loads of tables set out with people sitting and drinking tea and coffee and stuff. People in suits were reading big newspapers or talking with other people in suits. Everybody was so polite and helpful.

We've got our room 'til Monday. It's really big with a T.V. and a phone. Everything matches – the carpets, the curtains, the bedspreads. The little tables and chairs are all made from the same wood. They even have pictures in frames to make the place seem more like home. There aren't any ornaments – but I did find a Bible in my bedside table.

The bathroom is enormous and we don't have to share it with anybody else. It has white and black tiles, and one of them big baths with feet. There's a huge pile of thick white towels and dressing gowns. This must be what being rich is like. Every day must be like this – with somebody sorting stuff out for you, and everything always matching.

There is a menu next to the phone. We can even have food brought to the room if mam doesn't want to go down for dinner. I have my own small room that joins on to this one. I haven't unpacked any of my stuff yet.

My nanna said that "it's just a long weekend", and she gave me twenty pounds '*pocket money*' as we left the house. I'm going to keep it for when we get back.

If mam's up to it, we might go and do some shopping tomorrow. She says that we'll have to go in early, before it gets busy. I think she'd like to have a look at the bigger shops. She hasn't been through to Newcastle or Sunderland since dad left.

Some of the kids at school talk about the clothes and music shops in Newcastle. They come through on the express bus on a Saturday morning and spend all day just looking around the shops or sitting on 'the green'. It always sounds like such a waste of time. Maybe I should go and see if any of them are there. It'd be funny to see people from school at the weekend. It'd be like being on another Geography trip.

Mam wouldn't notice if I slipped out while she's asleep. The bed must be comfortable because she really struggles to sleep during the day at home. I wonder if I should go to my room and sort my stuff out. I've brought my pens and paper so I can write some letters or get my home-work done for Monday. I haven't got that much enthusiasm for school at the moment. I lie down and try to work out what I should do first.

The hotel room door bursts open and Brian comes dashing in.

"Quick – we need to get going!" My mam looks startled. Brian has woken her up. She doesn't ask any questions, though, so me and Brian help her into the wheel-chair. "We haven't got long," Brian says breathlessly, "they're waiting for us downstairs!" We spin out of the hotel room and into the corridor. Brian jabs at the buttons to call up the lift.

"What's going on?" I ask him, but he just grins and shakes his head.

"Don't worry – it's all taken care of."

Before we know it, we're in the hotel lobby, and we race to the main entrance. The staff smile and hold the doors wide open for us – almost as if they've been expecting us. The lobby is busy with people and their newspapers but they all stop to look as we pass through. Maybe I imagine it, but as we leave I'm sure I can hear everybody clapping and cheering.

Outside in the sunlight one of them big shiny four wheel drive cars stands waiting for us. The back windows are all blacked out and it looks as though it has private number plates: SAL 1000. In the front seats, there are two people – and they're both wearing Frankenstein monster masks. The Frankenstein in the passenger seat jumps out of the car and takes her mask off.

"Come on, Chris!" It's Nikki. She's beaming. "It's all sorted!" The other Frankenstein has also removed his mask, but I don't recognise him. "This is my boyfriend," Nikki explains. "Well, he's my ex-boyfriend, but we're still friends and he's offered to help us!"

Looking For Atlantis

The wheel-chair is safely stashed in the boot, and mam is seat-belted into the back of the car. Brian and I sit either side of her. Mam doesn't say anything, but her eyes are wide and she's smiling like I've never seen her smile before.

"We're all set!" Brian yells. The engine roars into life and the car weaves as we race through the streets of Newcastle. The buildings are much taller than they are in our town, and there are far more cars and buses clogging up the roads.

"Your plan worked brilliantly!" Nikki is breathless with excitement. "We didn't have any trouble – nobody tried to be a hero – we were in and out of the bank in less than two minutes!" And that's how I find out what's going on.

Sal turns the sound up on the car stereo. It's Prefab Sprout: 'Looking For Atlantis'. The music seems to make him drive faster. I look out of the back windows – nobody is following us – no Police, nothing. It's as if we're meant to get away with the money.

Paddy McAloon is singing. There are speakers all around us. It's like Prefab Sprout are actually in the car with us;

"You should be loving someone,
And you know who it must be,
'Cos you'll never find Atlantis,
'Til you make that someone me!"

Nikki turns around and looks at me through the gap between the front seats. She winks at me with those beautiful pale eyes. My mam either doesn't notice or decides not to say anything.

Before we know it, the car screeches to a halt at an airport. It's a wide open space, with planes landing and taking off all over the place. It's loud and it feels as if a strong wind is whipping around us.

The car doors are opened from the outside – and that's when I notice the crowd of people who have come to meet us. David, Janice ('her ladyship') Parky, Ollie, Adrian, Plettsy, Jacko, Faye, Paula, Nobby and everyone else from school is standing on the tarmac. They are all here. Mr. Mowatt shouts 'well done Chris!' Mr. Parr shakes my hand and slaps me on the shoulder. They are all smiling warmly. Even Mrs. Nixon has changed her cardigan for the occasion. My brother isn't there – he must still be busy with exams – he's the only one missing. Mam doesn't even mention him.

Brian emerges from the back of the car with the wheel-chair and a large black brief-case. He helps mam into the chair and presents her with the case.

"There should be more than enough there," he laughs, "more than enough. Just make sure you keep anything you have left over – there's a bloke outside of Woolworths who could do with a new Winter coat!"

David hands me two passports.

"How?" I ask him.

"My dad works at the passport office – he sorted them out in double quick time – and I paid for them with the money from the vending machines! It all worked - no problem!" I say thank you to him – I say thank you to everyone. We all yell to be heard over the sounds of the aircraft.

Mam and I are practically carried onto a waiting plane by a sea of smiling faces. As we reach the door-way, my nanna steps out in front of us. My heart skips a beat. Is she going to spoil it? Is she going to get up on her high horse and stop us from going?

"I read everything you wrote," she says, "I'm sorry but I did go through your desk and I hope you'll forgive me... We all decided to make this trip happen!" My nanna is smiling. In fact, she's smiling so much that I almost expect her false teeth to fall out. She kisses us both and then steps back to join the other well wishers. There is a huge round of applause as we board the plane.

Brian grabs my hand as if to shake it, but he presses a thin white rectangle into it instead.

"It's an MP3 player," he says, "I loaded every Prefab Sprout track I could find onto it – and some

*Morrissey!" I'm stunned. I'm stunned that people did listen to
the things I'd said. I'm just….*

*We take our seats, people bring us drinks, and my
mam is so happy that she's actually lost for words. There
aren't any other passengers on the plane, and the staff ask us
what films we want shown during the flight.*

*We're just about to get underway when Nikki dashes
up the aisle of the aeroplane. She leans in close to me and
whispers in my ear;*

*"Who said life doesn't have any happy endings?" She
kisses me gently on the cheek and says; "I'll be waiting for
you – when you get back!" And then she waves goodbye.*

*Mam and I put our seat-belts on and get ready for the
flight.*

"What the hell are you doing?" Mam is awake. "It's
bloody freezing in here!"

"I'm just looking at the view," I tell her, "you can see
right along the quayside!" The evening has come down, and
there are stars appearing above the bridges.

"And you're letting all the cold air in!"

"I've never seen the Tyne Bridge before."

"Don't be daft," she says, "it's always on the local
news."

"I mean, I've never seen it up close, in real life." I've
never been to Newcastle before.

"You've not missed much," mam says, "it's just
another big metal thing." She swings her feet onto the floor
and stands up as best she can. She sometimes does this at
home – she can walk across a room as long as there's enough
furniture to get hold of.

"It looks brilliant – all lit up." There are lights along
and around the curves and struts of the bridge. It looks like
there must be a non-stop stream of cars and buses and trucks
going across the Tyne Bridge. Lots of lights are moving
backwards and forwards all the time. I think about what this
view must have been like before they had the bridge and the

lights and the traffic. I wonder if William Wordsworth made it this far north and saw the stars at the mouth of the Tyne.

"It's just a bloody bridge." Mam takes one look and then struggles back to her bed. She picks up the TV remote control.

"It's a lot like Sydney Harbour Bridge," I want to tell my mam, "I think they copied the design." I'm sure I heard that somewhere. Maybe McPherson told us about it. Mam probably wouldn't be very pleased if I reminded her of Auntie Pat and Australia.

"If the TV has cable channels then you can watch last week's Search for a Pop Star again," I tell mam, "they repeat it every Friday night." She doesn't answer.

I ask her if she wants a cup of tea.

As I switch the kettle on and put the little tea-bags into the empty cups, I think about what Nikki said, that day in the dining hall. She said we can only do what we can do, and not get angry because life isn't fair and people don't help as much as they could. I think about my nanna and the money she's spent on letting us get away for the weekend. She must love my mam.

I've brought a little tape player with me – it's one of those old ones with big chunky buttons and only one speaker. I'm sitting on the bed in my little room playing some Prefab Sprout (*'We Let The Stars Go'* off the *'Jordan: The Comeback'* album) when I hear movement.

"What's that noise?" Mam is on her walking sticks, looking round the door at me.

"Sorry mam, did I disturb you?"

"Yes. Are you listening to those old songs again?"

"Yes, sorry... I'll turn them off..." I click the 'off' buttons.

"I don't know why you like all that stuff..." Mam has never talked about music with me before. "I haven't listened to any of it in years..."

Looking For Atlantis

"I kept all the records, from when..." I still can't bring myself to say the 'd' word.

"From when your dad left?" She wrinkles her nose when she mentions as him, as if she can smell something particularly nasty.

"Yes."

"He took all the ones he wanted, just left a few rubbishy old punk albums but I put those in the bin – the rest were mine."

"Eh?" I can't believe it. "So you liked Prefab Sprout?"

"Back then I did, yes. He had lovely eyes that Paddy McAloon. I saw him a couple of times at the City Hall in Newcastle. That was long before you came along." My mam loved Prefab Sprout. She *fancied* Paddy. She must've heard me listening to some of his songs a hundred times but she's never said anything 'til now.

"But I thought you only liked Bryan Adams and all those American blokes."

"You can like more than one thing, y'know Chris."

"Prefab Sprout records are my favourites," I say, "most of the kids at school think I'm daft for liking old stuff, but..."

"They're a bit soppy sometimes," she says, "and a bit too clever. I could never work out what he was on about half the time."

"But you used to like them."

"I used to like your dad. He used to go mad 'cos I wrote Paddy fan letters."

So we sit there, in our room looking out over the Tyne Bridge and we talk about Prefab Sprout. Mam tells me to rewind the tape and put it on again, from the very beginning. I know all the words to the songs and it's funny to think that she might too.

Mark Magrs

"Sure is good to seek a challenge,
Sure is fine to set your sights,
Sure is foolish to be blinded,
There are legions out there churchin'
Searchin' for the holy grail,
Isn't one of them can find it,
All this time..."

Reply from the Mayor Number 3

The Office of the Lord Mayor
Town Hall Chambers
21 – 25 Heighington Street

Dear Christopher,

Thank you very much for your letter. I have looked at your suggestions with a great deal of interest, and I will make sure that they are discussed at the next full meeting of the town council.

Yours sincerely

Theresa Rutter (Mrs.)